THE DECAMPION

York Aurel

VANTAGE PRESS
New York

This is a work of fiction. Any similarity between the names, characters, and places in this book and any real persons, living or dead, is purely coincidental.

FIRST EDITION

All rights reserved, including the right of reproduction in whole or in part in any form.

Copyright © 2004 by York Aurel

Published by Vantage Press, Inc.
419 Park Ave. South, New York, NY 10016

Manufactured in the United States of America
ISBN: 0-533-14848-0

Library of Congress Catalog Card No.: 2004090510

0 9 8 7 6 5 4 3 2 1

To my parents, Ezequiel and Teresa, the 'ciborium' where all my dreams emanated. And to my wife Carmen, and daughters Marta Helena and Yvonne Alicia, whose love helped me to accomplish this special dream.

Introduction

From home to work. From work to school. From school to the house..., by subway..., by bus..., I covered many miles, and spent many hours. When not busy with my own homework, or class-room lessons, I graded my students' papers....

Four days a week, for several years, I presided over groups of up to forty-seven mature individuals, teaching a specialized ten-month-long course, entitled: "Federal Communications Commission (FCC) License Preparation", in three sessions, to obtain the Third, the Second, and finally the First Class License in Electronics Engineering for Radio and Television stations' technicians. But during my days off, I concentrated on writing down my ideas for the production of books/motion pictures, in Science Fiction; Westerns; Adventure in Country Living; Criminal Court cases; love affairs, etc., etc., and tried to develop them ... up to a point.

Life's ups-and-downs dictate time and circumstances. Married life, and the upbringing of children (two gorgeous, intelligent girls, now both professionals), each exacts a toll on your energies and means; and the Muses 'vacation at your expense' during long periods in your life span! Indeed.

Time off ... however, was up, one day, and I returned to my ideas. Free of school-class lessons to learn, and of homework to grade, I dedicated my free time after work to expand my original dreams. No problem there! Rejection, criticism, was no deterrent. Except ... Like for most immigrants, English is usually a second language. Not that I spoke Spanish on a daily basis. Simply that I never studied the English language with the proper mentors. I did, of course, beg those I talked to, to correct my mistakes, and to teach me the proper way to say what I had just said . . . before they started 'candidly sniggering,' due to my bad pronunciation and/or my poor grammar structure. Unfortunately, however, not all my 'teachers' knew the right way. . . . What a shame!

Traveling around the country introduced me to different accents, and forms of expression. A very valuable tool for anyone trying to learn how to speak a foreign language. Although in the Armed Forces (I was a paratrooper serving in the U.S. Army, assigned to the Special Forces, "Green Berets," as a weapons specialist), where I had the opportunity to travel North, West and South, I met many North Americans (and aliens . . . I don't know from which worlds!!!) from as many geographical as well as ethnic backgrounds, who supposedly spoke English. . . . Their ways of expressing themselves, (those 'idioms!'), unfortunately, left me more perplexed than a parrot left inside of a corral full of hens along with their 'master' rooster! (If you catch my drift!!!)

But here I am! And, thanks to you . . . the readers of my book, *The Decampion*, I have finally become an author. By the way, my real name is Jorge Aurelio de Jesús Calderón Calderón (as in the name of Pedro Calderón de la Barca [1600–81], the Spanish dramatist) born and raised in the country of Colombia, S.A. There and then, one of my uncles on my mother's side, Alberto, also one of my elementary school teachers, used to call me "Mr. York" since I was six years of age. My friends in school always called me "York" throughout my teen-age years. (My uncle was fascinated with New York City, and love to read about life in America, in order to use his knowledge in the classroom.) And some of my Greek and Latin language teachers in the seminary schools I enrolled for high school and the Humanities studies, used to call me "York Aurelius." Hence, my 'pen-name' YORK AUREL!

For all of you who, like me, struggle daily not only as an immigrant to be able to fit in the country of our predilection, but as an American worker under the pressure of everyday life, I, the *Subway Writer* say 'Thank You,' and offer you to share some moments of my life, with the hope that my struggle gives you the incentive of—constructively—using your present to enhance your future, and the future of your children's children.

1

At the International Motion Picture offices where Nelson St★ had been working for some time as a regional manager of the Film to Tape Transfer Production Department and of the Film and Video Tape Distribution Center for the nation's theaters and major advertising agencies, the day shift employees were getting ready to go home. A last minute request from one movie theater operator from another state kept Nelson on the phone line a little bit longer than usual. It was on a Friday, eve of a three-day national holiday weekend.

"Next week we got to get together to discuss the new hours and shift schedules I mentioned to you before," said the general manager emphatically, glancing into Nelson's office after pushing the door with his elbow, while at the same time he was putting on his coat. Nelson, caught by surprise at the moment he was trying to write down a new client's address and telephone number, simply acknowledged with "Fine . . ." in a low voice. After a pause, he added, "Oh, by the way . . . ah, you . . . you did not give me the memo you said you had written for me."

"Oh yes! I forgot. We'll discuss that personally next week," answered the general manager. "See you after the weekend. Have a good one," he continued.

"Thank you. You too," said Nelson, grabbing his own coat and stepping out of his office to go down to the garage.

In his car, a two-door sport coupe, Nelson could easily cover the traveling distance between the building where he worked—a large and very luxurious office conglomerate built outside of town—and his own apartment, located not too far from the urban center, but on the old main road, away from the highway, and on the other side of town, in about twenty minutes. But Nelson usually drove out of his way to pass by the foot of the mountain standing majestically at the rear of this municipality, in order to contemplate it, and to meditate, while he reminisced about the most spectacular view he had ever observed. . . . The scene he had viewed while on his special trip to space earlier in his life! Yes. He still carried a mental picture of such a magnificent view, deeply buried in his memory and very close to his heart.

From the day Nelson had moved to this new location, and ever since seeing that mountain, his thoughts had always been linked to it, especially since his first attempt to escalate it had failed. Besides reminding him of that recent trek, the mountain constantly brought back memories of his childhood, especially during his days off from school, when he used to climb a very steep butte located near his place of birth, a hill he considered just a good facility for training exercises to stretch his muscles and to clear his mind from the heavy schedule of learning during the previous months.

But in reality, in Nelson's serious thoughts, this lofty mountain located in the background of his new town, seemed to be there not just like any other mountain in that region of the country. No way! For some special reason, Nelson saw it instead more as a monumental obstacle that reminded him, mentally, emotionally and physically, of a very special event in his existence. Consequently, it also became a challenge for him to conquer. Then, he could feel free, and have the drive to succeed, and the incentive to exist, in his second chance at a new life! Yes, indeed! This natural elevation is actually a typical "cordillera" remnant, a "picacho," having steep sides and a narrow but kind of flat summit. Just days after he had moved to the new town, Nelson had seriously attempted to climb the mountain, but he had been unsuccessful. He needed better training and more determination. *Perhaps some day!* he had constantly repeated to himself.

Nelson's neighborhood was a quiet, upper class, residential section. The building he owned was a modern, elegant structure with five floors, each containing four comfortable, large apartments, except for the first floor, which had only three: two regular size, and one double, the apartment Nelson (as landlord) occupied, with an independent entrance from the main door of the building. This extra facility gave direct access not only to the front garden but to the backyard. The garden and the backyard served Nelson's therapeutic needs as well as his special interest and compelling hobby, the growing of beautiful flowers, vegetables, and fruits during his spare time. The flowers were used to decorate his own apartment, also serving as models for his photography and painting studies, and as an elegant and delicate "introductory present" to every lovely woman he had the honor of meeting and the pleasure of knowing. The vegetables and the fruits, he consumed on a daily basis. Perhaps only psychologically, but all three—flowers, vegetables, and fruits—made him feel closer to Earth, and brought him, obviously, both pleasure and even luck. Besides, those were the two important promises he had made to himself, earlier in his life, when he was totally unable to be in direct contact with Mother Nature; the time he spent away from this world! But in spite of his daily office work where he kept his mind occupied for up to sixteen hours some days, and his occasional horticultural relaxation, his existence had actually become a tiresome routine.

Day after day coming home to an empty apartment had emphasized the pain and the loneliness he had felt for so long. Solace was an impossible dream. Nelson tried to occupy his mind by writing, and his body by sporadic exercise, but to no avail. He had already accepted the reality of his existence. Almost forty-seven years of age, totally out of shape (and, add to it) drinking wine more often than ever before in his life, Nelson nevertheless felt he owed himself another try at living! The name "Nelson St★," a name that had been given to him initially by a woman he did not know, but whose physiognomy, for some special reason, was constantly in his mind, had also constituted his identity during certain specific previous years between the ages of three (the time he received it) and eighteen. And now again the government, for national security reasons, had returned it to him at this specific time after he had come back, just a few months before, from his mission to space. (The name "York Aurel," his birth name as far as the government knew, had been given back to him again when he became eighteen, and he had kept it until the last day at the end of age forty-six, that is, through the time he worked for the government during his astronaut training years and his trek to space.)

About six months after his return from that space mission, his wife, son and two daughters had died in a mysterious car accident, denying him the chance to make up for lost time—the years he had spent during his trek to space as Commander York Aurel. This spatial mission had been kept top secret from start to end, from the entire world, from almost all relatives, from the press especially, and from all non absolutely essential personnel in the space travel business, with the exception of some very specially qualified high ranking officials in certain branches of the government. Now, Nelson's personal identity had been changed yet again to suit some strange government design he still did not comprehend. The records kept by the government, but never shared with any other person or agency, indicated that Nelson had been born on January 9, 1987 at an Indian reservation called Cristiania, located near a small village named Caramanta, in the southernmost tip of the Rocky Mountains, in a remote region of the state of New Mexico.

The records further indicated that he was the son of Eze-Ke-L and Teres (government employees themselves, with a very special mission to accomplish), who had named him York Aurel. Also, that at about the age of three his name had been changed to Nelson St★. Nelson precisely recalled traveling, on two different occasions, a long time ago, on a government plane, to the funerals of his real parents, whose loving faces he still remembered well. *He also remembers with some joy and with much appreciation for them, the look of all his foster parents, as well as the look of some of his friends from school. But what he remembers best is his vivid and extraordinarily rich childhood experiences that included not only the ones lived during school time, but mainly those that took place during vacation days at the end of the school year . . .*

Today's new job, however, in an industrial conglomerate owned by the family of an old time friend and military liaison (retired Commander Rœderick Blake, Ph.D. in Electronics Engineering, and offered to Nelson by the friend's relatives), served its purpose well at this particular time and during his present new living conditions. It was intended to help remedy Nelson's new and delicate personal situation: the transition between his old astronaut job and his new civilian life, especially after the loss of his entire family that had aggravated the circumstances. A kind of therapy prescribed by his old friend in arms. *But was it, really?*

Depressed for some time after the car crash death of his entire family, Nelson St★ had even considered committing suicide. Excessive drinking was, now, threatening to become a real problem; a problem a few close coworkers and acquaintances had already brought to his attention.

Alone most of the time, and unable to make new friends and to enjoy some time off with those who still cared for him, Nelson spent his free time either in the front garden, or in the vegetable-and-fruit patch located in the back yard, whenever the weather allowed. Watching television programs depicting nature, the performing arts, space and science, or attempting to write his memoirs, also occupied part of his time. Disappointed, however, by lack of interest on the part of some literary agents, he dreamed constantly, instead, of personally performing the quests achieved by the heroes whose lives were depicted in some of his books. (Nelson's personal life was, in fact, a science fiction adventure novel per se!) However, his solemn promise to the government, as an officer and a gentleman, to maintain total secrecy about his past professional experiences, did not allow him to become the best selling author he had hoped he could be!

At home this evening, after having changed into comfortable clothes, Nelson grabbed a well-chilled bottle of French white wine. Then he sat at his computer board and started to input a few sentences on chapter thirteen of his new project. A telephone call interrupted his line of thought. Getting up to look for the phone among the disarray on his desk, he cursed at the circumstances of his living conditions.

"Hello!" he shouted. Then, "Oh, I'm sorry," he apologized, recognizing the voice on the other side of the line. "How are you?" he added. "How is business?"

"I am afraid I have bad news for you, Mr. St★," said the voice on the phone. "They rejected your last idea. Sorry. Better luck next time! Goodbye."

Nelson had been waiting for quite a long time. The fame and fortune he hoped to one day achieve through success in writing were actually extremely difficult to obtain. Up to now a couple of his projects had been read by a literary agent whom he considered the best in the business, but who had not shown any interest whatsoever in publishing his work. Was the government in any way behind this? He had occasionally considered changing agents in the hope that he could find one whose point of view, different from that of his present representative, would trigger a positive reaction, and by doing so, one of his works at least would reach publication.

Unfortunately, none of his ideas had been viewed so far in the same light as he had presented them and wanted them to be viewed. Why? Although his agent had agreed that some of his work contained enough substance, and that a few of his ideas were excellent, Nelson had been told that he lacked concatenation, and that his rhetoric was too difficult for the average reader to comprehend. "For your type of genre," his agent had written, "and the age of the people who read it, you write well above average. Your imagination is amazing and your creativity is great. So you might have to consider using language more attractive to those you would like to become your readers, in order to establish your own following."

"What kind of nonsense is this?" was Nelson's reaction. As his exoneration, he confessed that, in reality, he had never written anything in a book style—always as a film treatment, hoping to go directly into the production of a motion picture. As people in the business know, a "treatment" is presented in the way the film should be shot. Although Nelson explained this to the editor he spoke to, his ideas were totally ignored. The only positive answer was that making a movie directly from one of those ideas would cost one hundred million dollars or more, a tag not too many producers could afford. *Was this a put down, or what? Honestly, considering the theme of his original idea, Nelson still believes that the government had indirectly acted against him, coercing the agent in such a way that he avoided proceeding with the publishing of Nelson's book and with the production of a motion picture, in order to try to conceal even more now his "spatial mission," for such a long time under wraps!*

Upset by the negative response and not really aware of his actions, Nelson turned on the TV. Then he went into the kitchen and prepared himself a sandwich. He rarely did this, but in special circumstances, like this one, he felt the need for one. He made a special type trying to imitate the kind of sandwich he ate from time to time when he visited a Hungarian friend whose Italian spouse was an expert gourmet. This was a hot pastrami and corned beef combination on seven-grain bread, with sweet green pickles alongside and a strong black beer to wash it down. Certainly a delicious and fulfilling meal to calm his anxiety!

Still uneasy, he walked around his apartment like a somnambulant, not knowing what to do. After a while Nelson finally sat in front of the TV to eat his sandwich. And while he attempted to do so, he mentally searched for something in his life, he did not really know what.

When he finally realized what he was looking for, he slowly got up and went to his closet, and looked desperately for a specially wrapped package. On TV the sports section of the nightly news was being broadcast. Oblivious to his own actions, Nelson removed the wrapping paper, opened the package and pulled out a gun, a .38 caliber revolver.

After looking at it for a long, long while, staring at it without even seeing it, he then, unconsciously, held the gun to his head.

But in spite of feeling desperately deep pain, Nelson nevertheless hesitated to pull the trigger; a strange and powerful force restrained him from carrying out what he considered the "relief" of his mental and emotional anguish. The photograph of his wife and children, still adorning the mantelpiece on his bedroom fireplace, commanded his full attention during those moments of intense suffering. But as if seeing their picture only with his soul, and with his heart all wrapped up into one excruciating sentiment of combined love for them and regret for his actions, his physical eyes seemed to have been induced to fix their sight exclusively on a circle occupying the space around all four faces, as if superimposed on the frame of the picture. It was as if an aura of glory was floating around them.

Meanwhile, Nelson's mind observed the concealed face of another person, the veiled nimbus image of "another woman" vaguely overlaying her physiognomy, like a transparency, over the faces of his family members, as in a long dissolve, in and out, double image scene in a film, without erasing the features of his lovely wife, the handsome boy and the two beautiful girls.

Nelson's subconscious mind and soul did register, though imperceptibly at this time, the message imprinted by the almost concealed face. Through the inner threads of his soul and mind passed, in an instant, his own life, and the lives of those he had loved so dearly and had lost so abruptly, making him perceive, now, the failure of his own existence, and filling with sorrow his own heart at this moment when he came to realize how far down he had descended morally, with his own actions. Looking around, however, without even seeing anything, he felt his entire body in a cold sweat and his face bathed in perspiration. Then he saw the trembling of his ice-cold hands. Reflecting for a moment, he put the gun aside and cried inconsolably.

It was the longest, coldest, darkest night of Nelson's forty-sixth year of existence. After falling into bed with his clothes still on, inebriated and only half conscious of having restlessly consumed several bottles of wine and beer, Nelson could not really fall asleep.

The clock indicated 1:56 A.M. The TV set was still on. As Nelson got up to put away the gun, a television commercial advertising the showing of the upcoming archival movie caught his eye. He placed the empty bottles in the garbage pail, and then, his mind at ease, sat down to watch the movie. It was an adventure drama in which the heroine mentally, emotionally, and physically "revives" her existence by bringing herself up from a deep depression produced by a life of loneliness and deception. In it she achieves the impossible: she participates in an important athletic event where the mind and the body are required to take the most painful abuse a human is willing to endure in search of glory, fame and fortune, during a single day's, three different sports, competition.

The story portrayed in that movie awoke Nelson's curiosity and made him evoke his youth as an athlete. It also made him reflect on his present existence and brought to mind the motion picture treatment he had written several years before, which he had put aside after being told by his agent that it "needed more work." The film depicted Nelson St★ as a winner of several competitions, a hero in the Olympics, defying all odds, while matching wits with the most famous, and with the best trained athletes of the world!

Nelson reacted to the film by subconsciously realizing, and by finally accepting, the fact that it was a clear expression of his own concept of the life he was living. Although his ambivalent existence had become an antidote to his mental anguish, loneliness was still Nelson's constant companion. He cried frequently, temporarily relieving his soul from the agony produced by the loss of his beloved family. Physically, Nelson at this point had given up almost completely. His body was soft and weak. Though his mental energy was high, it lacked nevertheless the necessary determination to compel his body to do even the least demanding physical exercise. Observing himself in the mirror, the only thing he saw was a flabby, overweight, lazy bum. But, as the saying goes, where there is a will, there is a way. If the woman in the movie could accomplish such prowess, why not him? Unfortunately, her deed, he reasoned, was only a 'make believe' story that could not really be used as an example. Futile excuse used to diminish the needed will power required for his own exoneration!

Days . . . weeks . . . passed. Winter had come and gone. In Nelson's mind there remained scenes of the film he had watched months before. He constantly thought about the film's theme of triumph over adversity, and the more he did, the more he pondered the possibilities of achieving the same proficiency by himself. Nelson was convinced that it had been meant for him to have watched that movie at that particular time, and under those specific circumstances. And so, as in a vision from the future, the explanation finally triggered his mind.

He now remembered that years before, amid the comforts of his home, and while he was still living among the people he loved most on this Earth, he had seen the real episode of the aforementioned event unfold in front of his own eyes during a re-run of a sports program on television, and that he had observed at the end of that competition the tragedy of a woman participant who had almost died, just yards before crossing the finish line. Nelson then realized that the film was in fact the vivid account of a true story. With such an example to follow, his mind was finally made up.

Looking at himself in the mirror again, this time he saw a totally different reflection. Instead of the tired, fat, flabby and lazy image of several months previous, he observed the future: an energetic, trim, well built, dynamic athlete—a winner. (By the way, spring had just returned, and with it, Nelson's new attitude in life.) From that moment on, Nelson's existence changed. Mentally, he returned to his youth. Emotionally, he accepted the tragic deaths of his family as a way of giving him a chance at a new life. Physically though, the situation was still very different. Fatter, heavier and lazier than ever, his body did not respond with the same agility his mind and heart had. Fortunately, at about the same time, Nelson's working hours were switched. With the new schedule he was able to allocate some time in the early morning to begin a personal training program. Twenty, thirty, forty-five minutes, one hour a day, started Nelson in the path to his hoped-for glory!

2

The summer days were longer. The warm weather gave Nelson the incentive to get up earlier every day, in order to stretch the total amount of time he wanted for exercise. And during the evening hours, to walk, in order to digest his late meal. During his daily constitutional, he revived in his mind the times he had spent as a young man training for his "utopian" Olympics . . . during which he would become "the champion of the world!" It is amazing how the mind can link certain events that are set apart by an entire life of rare circumstances.

For Nelson, the present day was practically the same as it had been over a quarter of a century before. The more he walked now, the more he improved in strength. The longer and more strenuously he exercised now, the more stamina he developed; but also, the more scared he became when he thought of the pain and suffering he would have to inflict on his body, at this late time in life, in order to achieve success. Yet, knowing that a final triumph demands middle-of-the-road defeats, he pushed harder and harder, for longer hours, practicing different sports, convinced that a couple of years from then he could become an Olympic medalist. *Was Nelson just daydreaming, perhaps?* He did realize that his training would have to be not only improved under professional direction if he expected to win, but be diversified as to include, besides swimming, running the marathon, performing gymnastics, etc.—every single sports competition of the decathlon, in which he specifically, dreamed to compete.

With that thought in mind Nelson took immediately

the necessary steps. First, he needed to insure his inclusion as a participant in any of the member teams registered under the International Olympic Commission's authority. Second, as part of his motto: *Mens sana in corpore sano,* he then set out to change the circumstances of his living, deciding to stop his frequent libations (even if they were in honor of the Olympian gods). He began redecorating his apartment completely, setting up a rigid exercise schedule in his newly built gymnasium, in order to work out without interruptions. Although he foresaw obstacles and difficulties that made him, at first, doubt his chances of success, nevertheless, from that day on, Nelson promised himself never again to give up.

In a large city nearby, during the fall, a handsome six feet, two inches tall, fair complexioned, green eyed, brown haired, almost forty-seven-year-young, athletic man applied in person at the Olympic Committee Regional Headquarters for a chance to compete representing "his own world." For several months he had tried to obtain an answer to his written inquiries, but had only received one postponement after another for a personal appearance to contest his case. After a long wait, during which he realized that many later applicants had already been interviewed ahead of him, Nelson St★ was finally given the time he needed to express his intentions.

However, the single sentence: ". . . wishing to participate . . ." called the attention of the officials due not only to the fact that Nelson was much older than the usual applicants, but because of the unusual request (already on record), that he wanted to represent "his own world!"

Although some committee members believed that Nelson's age and his specific type of request did not meet the Olympic standards, they did not imply either that his request for participation could not be accepted. Asking him to wait a little while longer, the officials retired to discuss the situation further, before giving him any answers. Some time afterward, Nelson was informed that an official reply would be mailed to him at the earliest possible date. Disappointed, he felt that he absolutely had been unable to accomplish anything. What a waste of time and energy!

In spite of the excessive red tape, and aware besides of the short days that winter brings, Nelson continued with his training. In fact, he redoubled his efforts. Day after day his biking, swimming, jogging exercises, gave him the hope that one day soon he would receive the invitation he was looking for. Checking the mail box every morning, noon and evening, proved futile for a very long time. Still, he hoped to receive a prompt and a positive answer.

When this was not forthcoming, Nelson decided to write to the National Olympic Committees of several countries, offering to represent them, and requesting their support. To his consternation, some flatly denied him their help. And most actually ignored him completely. Not a single country offered him any support!

Many weeks passed. Finally, one early spring day while Nelson was doing some chores in the backyard, a special delivery letter arrived. Avidly, Nelson opened it. The message from his country was concise. "Your timing forbids the Committee to consent to your participation as a member of our nation's team. However, complying with international regulations, the National Committee promises to send your application to the International Headquarters suggesting that you be allowed to compete, but on the condition that you obtain sponsorship from 'somebody in the universe,'" it said. He was demoralized. To Nelson, this was not just a mock letter. In his view, what they had really meant was that he had been deemed too old to participate, without even having the chance to demonstrate his abilities or to show his potential to become a winner. *Was he right to make that assumption? Perhaps!* What was certain, though, was that the committee's statement comprised the feeling, and delivered the decision, taken by every nation.

At first, Nelson's reaction to his disappointment was the peaceful and calm behavior of the disciplined athlete. *Oh well, most participants have already been pre-selected by their own countries, anyway.* However, in the evening, while dressing to go out, the bad news really sank deeply into his heart. Tears ran down his cheeks. Upset, he began to throw things around. He slammed every door he passed by. Mentally fixed on "doing something," he picked up his gun again. But scared, he dropped it fast and grabbed a brand new bottle of scotch instead.

He then sat down to swallow the contents. Uneasily, he picked up the gun once again, and walked around his apartment while mumbling to himself, "Too old to participate! Too old to participate!"

He kicked things. He shook heavy furniture. He broke anything in his way. He made the ground tremble at each step he took. In reality, he felt he might be at the threshold of insanity! His loneliness; the memory of his beloved family; the pain produced by their loss still profoundly embedded in his heart, added to his constant mental anguish; the recollection of his past "literary" failure still rumbling in his brain—all were conjured up by this brand new setback, and his soul was downloaded as it had never been before. Looking at himself in the mirror for a long, long time while holding the gun in his hand, he finally realized the seriousness of his situation and the implications and consequences of his actions, and before continuing the battle against himself, he collapsed to his knees. Then, crying as a child in pain, he threw the gun against the mirror hanging in the dining room. The mirror broke into a thousand pieces. And without thinking twice, Nelson left the apartment with the half-empty bottle of scotch still in his hands, closing the door behind him with a bang.

Nelson had not expected such an inflexible blow to his ambition. The drawback he had experienced had made him, in spite of his early decision, temporarily drop out of the race against himself and against his depression, and had taken him back to where he had first started. Alone, he looked for solace some place else! Curiously, during the last moments before leaving his apartment, the ghost face of that woman he had "seen" before, had formed a profound impression again in his subconscious mind, right at the time the mirror was being crushed. It was as if the broken pieces had assembled momentarily once more to form a mosaic of the lady's face before crashing down, and before they were spread all over his apartment floor.

It was a rainy, hot, humid, spring night. Like a somnambulant, Nelson paced the streets of his town without regard for his disheveled appearance, and paying no attention to the looks and comments of passersby. Not too many people knew who he was anyway. Some had heard of him and of his adventures in space, but could not attest to the rumors. A few were mere acquaintances, but spoke only out of courtesy, with only a simple, sporadic greeting as the whole conversation. He kept mainly to himself. His countenance, and the strength of his character, combined with the mental energy that always radiated from his presence, deterred many from becoming his personal friends, and did not allow him to surround himself with anybody else who did not measure up to his high standards. Although he enjoyed the momentary company of decent individuals, he could not accept those persons without any basic manners or lacking proper hygiene, as well as those who constantly used foul language in order to emphasize what otherwise they could not express. Willing to listen and able to discuss any serious subject matter in several languages, he could not waste time on any project without a specific constructive purpose. Always with a good disposition, though, and extremely polite, Nelson was not the type of person however who allowed anyone to get close to him. His mind was always at work, either reminiscing about his past, or speculating on a nebulous future project. He had no time for trivialities. An excellent instructor, detail oriented, he was a motivational teacher; an educator who enjoyed helping others to amend errors spoken either in their own mother tongue or while learning and trying to cope using a second language, without the least intention of demeaning anyone in the process. But with the personal secret he had to keep in his soul, and the burden of the constant thought of the tragic death of his beloved family, there was no space in his heart for any small talk! Do not underestimate Nelson, however. His goodness of heart; his respect for humble persons; his admiration for those who thrived under the adverse conditions and circumstances that life brings, as well as for anybody with a brain and willing to use it for the benefit of others, made him a recipient of noble deeds.

Engrossed in his own thoughts, after an hour or so Nelson finally reached the outskirts of the city, where a police car was parked at a corner. The two officers inside were eating sandwiches and drinking coffee. When one of the officers observed Nelson, he asked the other: "Look who's coming! I wonder what the heck is he doing around here at this hour?"

After observing Nelson, and while chewing on his food, the other officer answered: "Oh, yeah. The athlete who wants to compete in the Olympics. I have heard that he is an astronaut who traveled to Mars or some place in space. Hah! In my opinion, I think he is just an 'astro*nut*,' if you ask me!"

Pausing to sip his coffee, he then added: "He trains at night sometimes, or very early in the morning." The first officer then remarked: "He looks like hell. Should we pick him up?" At this point a screeching voice came through the police car's radio with a call about a disturbance nearby. Both officers left immediately, letting Nelson continue his walk down the street.

Still drinking from the bottle of scotch he had taken from his apartment, Nelson instinctively started walking toward the mountain which he had unsuccessfully attempted to climb during several of his hiking trips while routine training, and which constantly reminded him of the cordillera's sector where he as a boy had seen the flames that kept on showing in his dreams, along with the face of the woman he had often seen as a ghost.

Perspiration ran down his entire body. His street clothes became uncomfortable. Tossing the bottle away after the last sip, he removed his tie and shirt, and kicked off his leather shoes. Resembling a derelict, with bloodshot eyes and naked upper torso, Nelson St★, face to face with the mountain, defiantly looked up, and after letting out a lion's roar of combined pain and rage, he swore to conquer its summit if that was the last thing he ever did!

Nelson stood there for a very long time. Inebriated as he was, he needed to pull himself together and adjust his mental state in order to be able to produce the decision needed for such an impossible task. Was he going mad!? Drinking in desperation, combined with the previous deceptions, had awakened in him not only pain and suffering, but outrage.

By contrast, the mountain itself was calm. It simply stood there in silence, embedded in the stillness of the night, producing its own darkness by spreading its shadows all around. Its massive swelling, a Mother Earth's monument to endurance, a lesson to the impetuous. A clear sky, with only a few menacing dark clouds left behind after the rain had subsided, advertised a change in the atmosphere. And the moon above, let out for the night, full and bright now as a silver dollar with a face of contempt, peeked at the living on the ground with one eye open, while blinking with the other every once in a while at the passing of the flying clouds.

The air was now dry, there was no wind. Besides her (his beloved, and at the same time hated, mountain) for company in such distressful moments in his life, Nelson felt totally alone . . . and in the middle of nowhere. That was what he reflected on, and what he started to believe.

However, subconsciously encouraging himself, he spoke aloud to the mountain, saying: "Yeah! Yeah! Yeah! I have never been able to set foot on you before, but that doesn't mean forever! Tonight is my night, and like it or not, this time I will not be defeated."

With strong determination then he started his ascent, perhaps not fully realizing the difficulty of the task ahead of him. Groaning and slipping often, he fell frequently. Lying on his back for minutes at a time, he recovered from his exhausting effort while mentally and emotionally he fought against a desire to quit before he could reach the top. Rocks and debris fell on him. Dirt and sweat went into his eyes, blinding him momentarily. Almost at the end of his climb, tired and weak, Nelson slithered once again, this time hurting himself and barely avoiding a fatal fall by just grasping and holding the roots of a dry bush. Blood spilled from hands, elbows, knees and feet, covering the rocks. His sweat washed it away. Tapping into his most inner energy sources, and with the determination of a conqueror, Nelson, breathlessly, finally climbed all the way to the highest peak.

His bloody feet did not even feel the cuts from the rocks forming the steps of the natural stairway of the terrain, all the way to the top. Looking at his badly bruised hands and feet did remind him though of his painful self-deception. At this time a sudden mental flash, the image of that same woman he had subconsciously noticed when he had broken the mirror, returned to his mind. *Funny*, he thought, the same flash of the same woman he had seen before as a halo surrounding the photographs of his wife, his daughters and son, had hit his mind again. Funny, because it recalled the face of that ghost person he was sure he knew but whose ID he could not recognize. But in such a stressful moment it was a revitalizing thought that pierced his soul and sent an electric shock wave through his entire body, giving his mind the needed energy for that last effort to stand up, and that kept him on his feet long enough to be able to observe the quiet town below. He enjoyed the view for a very long time. Looking down from above gave Nelson a great deal of satisfaction and, unable to control his emotion, he cried, this time for joy. . . .

Exhausted, he then collapsed; but only after having tasted the flavor of his victory for a little while longer by observing for the very first time the town's lights, from the highest point of his now cherished mountain. Unfortunately, in the same way everything in life is temporary, small pleasures don't last long.

The outpouring of his energy; the altitude; the chilly spring night's dew; his drinking; and his emotional devastation, had all combined to produce in Nelson St★ a rare reaction; he finally passed out.

Still in the twilight of his consciousness, and just before losing contact with reality, Nelson noticed that a searching light had suddenly appeared in the skies, flooding his body with powerful rays of brilliant colors. In his subconscious mind were imprinted—at least temporarily—the flashes emanating from above. During those moments, slowly, his mind went back to the place he had always remembered since he was a small child, the place where he had seen himself "totally surrounded by fire." And now, as in a repetition of his childhood experience, he saw himself again, this time surrounded by several strange looking beings. Mist rising from the wet grass covered with rime, clouded his body in all directions. Although he was semiconscious, a message was clearly recorded in his mind, a message he associated with the one he had received earlier when he had seen the image of that spectral woman dissolving into and out of the images of his dear family, in the picture on the mantel in his bedroom. A message in which Nelson was given the answer to his prayers!

As if hypnotized, he then found himself in the middle of a circle formed by several individuals whose faces were covered with masks of different shapes and colors. Still mesmerized, Nelson mentally asked while forcing his eyes to pierce the light shining on him: "Am I dreaming?"

"No. You are not," answered one of the beings in an exchange of telepathic waves, simulating a convincing but gentle human voice, and adding: "You are now among friends. Please do not worry. We are here to take care of you."

And after a long pause: "And, who are you, if I may ask?" said Nelson.

"We have come to Earth searching for perfect biological samples of human beings willing to share their genes with the best exponents from our own race, and other galactic races, in order to augment our depleted civilizations," replied the surreal being.

A second being then spoke while Nelson looked around in awe, trying to identify his location. "We are all aware of your desire to compete in the Olympic Games and of your wish to win the decathlon competition in particular. We are also conscious of your human age limitations and of your physical shortcomings. We not only have the ability to read your thoughts; we are also able to foresee your future. We would like to help you!"

"What am I to do?" interrupted Nelson.

"Just continue with your training in the manner you have been doing it up to now. We will soon visit you in your home. And from now on, some of us will be with you at all times as your trainers and helpers, and will give you the necessary support to not only compete, but to win!"

Another being then continued: "You must force yourself and try harder in order to achieve the results you set out to obtain. Your own determination, self control and will power, along with your training, will give you the stamina needed to endure the most demanding tests. Now, go back to your daily life and keep up with your every day routine work-outs. We will be with you at all times, even when you cannot see us." Nelson, astounded, said: "What's to happen then?"

"Well, we will go with you at the time of the final selection and, as representatives of all the beings from the universe outside of Earth, we will sponsor you!" answered the third being.

Fog had now completely covered the mountain. Returning to consciousness with a brutal headache, Nelson did not remember where he was at that time. Blaming his pain for his lack of coordination, he could not remember what had happened. Little by little, however, his mind started to unfold its inner threads, and the memory of the beings advising him about his Olympic aspirations finally returned. Subconsciously of course, he believed that such an encounter could have occurred only as a nightmare, probably from the effects of the alcohol he had consumed.

Vaguely conscious then, recalling the words from those beings, and happy with the outcome despite the fact that he believed that what had happened had been just a dream, he retraced his path down the mountain with his heart overcharged with happiness and his mind full of good thoughts, planning his athletic victories and convinced that finally, he could make those dreams come true. He was certain—no, he was thrilled—that nothing could stop him now. In his mind he pictured many glorious moments for himself as the winner of several competitions, and the idol of the multitudes. In his heart, the "utopian" Olympics of his childhood dreams were now one step closer to becoming his lifetime reality!

Since no one so far had believed that he was going to be able to compete, and since no country on Earth had accepted him yet, Nelson did not expect to have any try-outs in order to determine his abilities as a competitor. His training then, however, resumed with more vigor than ever. People loved to observe Nelson during his work-out routine. Exercises everyone judged to be excessively arduous for his age were considered by him only good enough to make him a champ. From that moment on, the lonelier Nelson felt while he was training, the larger the crowds he imagined would be acclaiming him with cheers at the Olympics!

3

Dreams recall experiences. Embedded in our memory is the past. There are many who believe that there are extraterrestrial beings living among us on this Earth, beings that are occupying not only space, but bodies of other humans, who either died or for obvious reasons disappeared. The popping on and off, in and out, by an alien being in a crowded street, at the bending of a corner, or suddenly appearing in the middle of some confusing circumstances, like the scene of an accident, a catastrophe, or among spectators of a sports event, where no one can immediately be aware of his or her existence, is nothing out of this world, as the understatement of the century would put it! Believing in the existence of aliens without any mental reservation connotes the acceptance of their superiority and of their extraordinary abilities. It also makes it easy for humans to comprehend their idiosyncratic ways of living among us. Thousands of unidentified flying objects (UFOs) have been reported in Earth's skies through the years. Missing persons' files keep increasing without any hope of finding those individuals. Accidents have been reported where "no survivors" were ever found and where bodies were never either properly identified, or totally accounted for. These reports fill thick folders in the computerized archives of human history.

All these concepts and opinions form only the negative part of the spectrum. What about the many prodigies in all kinds of intellectual and artistic endeavors who seem otherwise out of place on this Earth? Could it be that their mental power is actually the one received from another, far superior being who has taken possession of his or her body, and/or mind? And in the field of sports, or for that matter the heroes in the armed forces and related units in the service of humanity, where human endurance is tested well beyond a body's capability—doesn't it strike us as a little odd that only a few have the capacity to become great? If we are to take into account human frailties and how close to the beasts we humans still are, one has to ponder the possibility that at least *some* of our best achievements could have been dictated by a more sophisticated race than ours (without deducting anything, of course, from human ingenuity).

Little by little come to life astonishing achievements by scientists. A little too early for humanity? Perhaps at a time and during circumstances that hold no ground for adequate applications? Isn't it possible that, perhaps, what humans consider a new discovery, has for millennia been in the most recondite labyrinths of the human mind, mixed in the complex structure of our DNA; placed there by our ancestral founders, from other parts of the universe, who had already discovered those portents of science, and had perfected them, and their applications, before handing them down as legacy to humans? And that those same achievements are simply recollections by our memory, invoked by dreams, to be made into reality? This is not a denial of the human race's intrinsic power to create. It is a simple theorem pondering the inexplicable, as a solution to our own questions. As Plato's doctrine explains it: "Reminiscence is the theory of the recovery of things known to the soul in previous existences."

Lower class animals, those forming part of the commonly named lower species, bees, birds and ants, to name just a few, are capable of splendorous physical and scientific work, such as beehives, nests and underground fortresses. Still, it is impossible for humans to fully know and totally understand them; but, what is even worse, humans constantly and purposely destroy them and their habitats. It has been proven beyond any doubt, time and time again, that it takes a really superior being to comprehend what is commonly considered expendable by human intolerance and lack of human intellectual capacity. So, why not give here and now some of the credit due to those superior beings?

Finally the time came when the Olympic Committee had to make a decision about the finalists and their sponsoring countries, and Nelson St★ wanted to make sure that he was registered. Still apprehensive about his acceptance but for some obscure reason totally certain of a final victory, he did not even hesitate for an instant at the possibility of having to face again those same members of the Olympic Committee who had previously turned him down. In his subconscious remained the "dream" he thought he had on the mountain top. In it, now, it was not just a nation but an entirely yet unknown universe, which would be sponsoring him all the way to a complete triumph! Perhaps Nelson was convinced by what he thought was an apparition, that a strange but powerful force had given him lately the needed energy to improve on his training. And that now that same force was conducive to decide his preference for sponsorship. So when the members of the Committee asked him for the name of the country he was going to represent, his statement simply was: "Peoples from the Universe Outside of Earth!"

Unfortunately, some of the members of the Committee and of the press as well, caught by surprise at such an answer, couldn't help but laugh at what was considered to be a joke even by some of the officials. What they did not laugh about, though, was at the sudden appearance on the premises—seconds later, and out of thin air—of several individuals who identified themselves as Nelson St★'s "trainers and helpers." Dressed in sporting but elegant, sober but colorful suits and wearing matching eyeglasses, they gave the impression of being definitely "out of this world!" Their serious countenance, adding importance to their already distinguished natural appearance, and their fashionable appeal, conveyed more than a professional look. They left behind the image commonly projected by specially selected government enforcement officers, well-trained private eyes, and/or of members of a restricted and a very rich and powerful think tank organization. Obviously there was nothing really different about them as far as everyone present was concerned, except a certain "air . . ." which even in Nelson's opinion indicated an absence of . . . belonging. However strange the circumstances of their presence were, and the way these beings came across, different from other humans, they did not arouse any particular suspicion, nor did they prompt any questions or comments out of the ordinary. They were simply ignored with silent stares at their faces and absent-minded looks into their eyes, as if that were the appropriate thing to do at the time. Was that perhaps (telepathically speaking) their "dictated" attitude of mind? Unfortunately, in spite of Nelson's credentials, and after some discussion among a few of the Olympic Committee's members, his request was again denied for "lack of proper sponsorship." Fortunately though, a few press representatives and media reporters present at that moment had caught a glimpse of Nelson's face showing his predicament, and his story was circulated almost immediately. Public awareness of the Committee's turndown became Nelson's helping hand. Human rights groups and individuals' freedom of choice advocates were enthusiastically fired up by the media's account of a "one man team against the bureaucratic red tape of powerful organizations." They vociferously demanded from the Olympic Committee the acceptance of Nelson St★ as a true representative of "those peoples from the rest of the universe unknown to Earth!"

Even skeptics about UFOs and of ET theories spoke out in favor of Nelson St★. The force of sign-holding demonstrators, plus those who were demanding that Nelson be allowed to participate, carried their will and desire further than Nelson could have ever imagined. Volunteer professionals offered free legal services; a judicial battle was threatened. The Olympic Commission refused arbitration. A court hearing was scheduled. The argument? Since Earth's peoples cannot prove beyond a reasonable doubt that "aliens" (meaning extraterrestrials) do *not* exist, the just conclusion was to accept that they really *do*. Furthermore, it was agreed that Nelson had a right to have "them" as his "patrons" and consequently that he should be allowed to participate in the Games as a "One Person Team."

Nelson knew in his heart that eventually things would turn out for the best. He understood that due to the new circumstances, no matter what was the outcome, he would now have to endure every rigorous athletic test he had not been required to perform before. And that from now on, he would have to abide by every rule and regulation, which he was ready, willing, and able to do. He also felt that he was up to it in spite of all the tribulations this new way of doing things would bring him. Most importantly, he knew that he was "in" and consequently, he was happy!

The court session opened to hear Nelson's case under very strict security measures. This was done in order to counterbalance the "following" that the advance publicity had stirred up in Nelson's favor, and in spite of the fact that the presiding judge was a man whose reputation for helping lost causes had preceded him. The newspapers were also filled with front page articles depicting Nelson's ideals, along with fans' quotations, actually stating their personal reasons why they believed the problem was simply a total lack of interest on the part of the Olympic Commission in accepting him. On the streets however, supporters of the "freedom of choice" doctrine kept on demonstrating, not only advocating, but demanding the admission of Nelson St★ as a participant in the Olympics, and the acceptance of aliens as his sponsors. The crowd which had gathered in front of the court building (many of them dressed in extraterrestrial looking attire to depict their views . . . of the "out of this world" beings) kept on shouting their opinion, while television and radio crews interviewed on the spot anyone who seemed relevant to the case. Inside, however, a different situation altogether was unfolding. Although it was only a hearing, the parties debating Nelson's case went at each other's throats with the full strength of a court battle, impregnating the procedures with an air of discrimination, not only due to the age of the plaintiff, but to the fact that those who were supposed to become his backers were not even accepted as real! Nelson even carried his own sign: "JURISPRUDENCE IS NOT ALWAYS BASED ONLY ON EVIDENCE. LACK OF EVIDENCE IS ENOUGH TO MAKE A CASE!" The court was filled with reporters; curious fans; government agents; radical members of private organizations dedicated to the search for extraterrestrial life, and sleuthhounds backed by scientific societies hoping to uncover ETs living on Earth. All were eager to give testimony of their own encounters, along with representatives from the IOC subpoenaed to bring along a decision about Nelson's participation in the Olympics that would justify this such hearing.

Among those who claimed to be Nelson St★'s trainers and helpers, and the rest of the spectators accepted by the judge to be present at these procedures, there was discerned one, a woman who simply sat quietly in the court room without adding or subtracting anything to the course of action. The only person who actually noticed her was Nelson. And Nelson, not fully aware of his actions, kept staring at her every chance he had without fully understanding why. Obviously, he was simply intrigued by the woman's facial resemblance to that woman he subconsciously had seen twice before as a ghost image forming the background over and around the faces in the photograph of his wife, daughters and son.

Regrettably, Nelson's court case opened a big question about his personality and background, that kept the press avidly searching for him. News items about the reasons for his court appearance and in particular about his personal life, appeared by the dozen. His personal popularity soared. In addition, some sources of the news media saturated the world with alleged "stories" of his past and with his unreasonable plans for the Olympics. Realistic or not, and in spite of the annoyance that all this fuss had brought him, Nelson still was happy. Happiness, however, is a very short lived emotional state!

There were many unanswered questions concerning Nelson's life, personality and background. So, in an effort to identify him properly, Nelson's ancestry became the subject of intense investigation. Private organizations, along with the Olympic Committee and a government agency's branch of the missing persons' bureau (just to keep the secret under tabs), united efforts to find out Nelson St★'s real background. No one (supposedly) knew who he really was! Whatever sketchy records were revealed simply showed that the place he claimed to have come from, had been burned down years before. And that nobody knew him there anyway.

In a remote village, far, far away from the center of activities where the Olympic Games were to be played, and from the town where these court procedures were actually happening, Nelson's birth and childhood were placed under scrutiny. Numerous individuals claiming to represent the interests of both private agencies and of official government offices, descended upon the small town to try to uncover the real truth. Television, radio and newspaper crews set up shop for weeks. A handful of witnesses of events that happened at the time Nelson was a child, gave totally different accounts. Living testimony of the disaster that had occurred a few years after the time Nelson was supposed to have been born, did agree on one fact, however; the fact that all records had been lost in a horrible fire at the electrical plant. The fire had consumed the church, the parish house, the orphanage, the town hall, the school, and several blocks of residences forming the upper class neighborhood behind the main plaza. Many lives—both of children and adults—had been lost in that fire. But investigators were unable to see any evidence, pro or con, about the statement of fact offered by the remaining few who supposedly had witnessed the fire. And at the end, no clear picture came out of the search for the truth concerning Nelson's genealogical origins, or even his true place of birth.

Weeks before his third birthday, and during the celebration of the town's tercentenary festivities, a furious fire had started when some fireworks burst into flames inside the repair shop in the electrical plant while work was being done on a spark-generator. It had burnt about seventy per cent of the village, destroying everything in its path. What a tragedy! But was this really what happened? *Did anyone know the real truth?* And if they did, were they telling it? The explanation given concerning the fireworks fit the circumstances and the times, but did it fit the actual findings by the specialized team of government investigators?

Fireworks, of course, were the typical way for the town's folks to demonstrate their feelings for tradition.

Tragically though, those same fireworks they had loved and enjoyed so much and for such a long time, had actually become the regrettable cause of the devastation. Fireworks also have remained, as a consequence, since that particular day (so they still say), a permanent and invisible pyrotechnic epitaph to the memory of those who had perished. At the same time, they have marked the beginning of a new era for the people in the region. Although decorating the skies with beautiful lights represented their feelings, and was only supposed to warm their hearts, never again would be a display of such dangerous festive euphoria allowed to take place in that town. Total restrictions had been imposed eliminating the use of fireworks. And consequently, their danger forever!

The precious lives lost and the property destroyed, among which were relics of incalculable value and ancestral pride, barely compared with the agony suffered by those who remained behind. Their lives were ruined not only emotionally, but economically, civically and socially, as well. The obliteration of all records detailing their ancestry produced for many, in addition, an unavoidable lasting conflict. Their existence was changed radically, for without birth and/or marriage records to prove otherwise, their civil status was never again readily accessible. Lack of personal identification created other situations that caused further losses and jeopardized in many ways their future life. Those who were able to find people who could identify them, were lucky. Most—among them Nelson—did not have anyone who could attest to the facts of their existence. Like a pariah, Nelson went through most of his childhood and youth without knowing his true identity. Placed with foster parents, he was moved from town to town, home to home, until he was old enough to obtain his own ID in the form of an international passport offered to him by the American government, along with an open invitation to reside wherever he pleased, and with an offer for a full scholarship at the school of his choice—but with the condition to remain under the government's auspices until he reached the age of total legal independence.

Orphaned as a child, he remained so for many years, experiencing the painful loss of a family every time he was assigned to a new set of foster parents. As he grew to adulthood, one town after another hosted his puberty. During his early teenage years, and while he was still under governmental supervision, his custodial existence was finally ended. He had spent his childhood at several different private institutes under various scholarships, some of which were offered by religious organizations secretly supported by funds from the federal government, but channeled through state and municipal activities. Then, moved by some strange force that allowed him to "see" far into the future, Nelson took advantage of the offer included with his passport, and the trip to the town of his predilection was finally arranged. Nelson then went to reside in a very nice city that provided him with higher education and scientific work, along with a steady and a very generous income. (Due to his extreme precocity, Nelson had skipped a couple of years of basic primary and secondary education, and he had actually finished college long before the time he was supposed to have graduated from high school.)

Then, in that new town, and after a few more years of advanced education and specialized training, in the middle of worldly comforts and still at a very young age but with a highly developed and mature mind, he formed the family he had loved and cherished but had so tragically lost!

Government officials, IOC members and reporters descended like vultures into the old section of town, where Nelson St★ had lived as a child. That part of the town had been kept separate from the newly built one. Rumors circulated that something strange was buried under a specific section of the old town, which was now maintained as a park by the Department of Agriculture with restricted entrance to the public. It was an area where special trees and flowers were grown, and where from time to time some "experts" were seen taking readings off the land. . . . But nobody knew what really was under the green grass or under the heavy rocks adorning the grounds as so-called "natural" monuments to the past! Records were turned upside down in a frantic effort to find any trace of Nelson's real origins. For days these private investigators questioned everyone who could have any clues about Nelson's birth and/or his early childhood. Unfortunately, not a single person seemed to have any recollection of the boy's early life. And to make things worse, only a few were old enough to remember the day the town became an inferno. Church and police records were the most accurate account of the fire disaster, but neither showed any trace of Nelson St★'s existence.

Among the people interviewed, however, there was one woman who seemed aware of the facts as if she had been an eyewitness. She was the person in charge of the town archives, a kind of civic librarian—a type of job that many of the investigators found inconsistent with the size of the town, its administration and its budget. Her offices occupied part of her own personal accommodations. According to this woman, a child of Nelson's description had been originally placed in a foster home with a mature couple who lived in the outskirts of a nearby town and who had come to visit for the holidays. Unfortunately no one had seen this couple again since that day. She was probably concealing the fact that those folks were Nelson's real parents whom the government had finally identified and who were originally selected as his real guardians, in spite of the fact that he had been sent to other foster homes sporadically. Is it possible that Nelson was ever aware of that? Probably, because he did remember them. *Odd, to say the least.* Odd because when this woman's photograph was shown to Nelson by one of the reporters, days later, he could not comprehend why a person with such striking similarity to the lady he had seen several times as a ghost during the last few months would be occupying such a job, at such a time and in such a place.

But, going back to the inspectors, the so-called sleuths reported to their organizations that nothing substantial had actually been found about Nelson St★ and, ignoring those circumstances as the result of this small town's lack of interest and concern for outsiders, they proceeded to abandon the project. Of course, the branch of government that had granted Nelson his international passport, had previously done its own investigation, and had come up with its own identification, based not only on the information some reporters already knew, but also on facts relating to his life as a teenager, and as a student in the different schools of learning he had attended. Naturally, the intelligent and rich people in charge of the office that represented the most powerful country on Earth, had not only taken care of those who had any previous connection with Nelson, but had ensured that no one else—ever!!!—was going to be able to find out absolutely anything about this special boy they had found so fascinating!

From the mystery woman, however, reporters were able to gather that a child whose age, name and family lineage were totally unknown, had indeed been rescued from the ashes of the fire. Actually, the information she supplied was that a small boy approximately three years old, with a fair complexion, green eyes and long curly blond hair had, miraculously, come out of the flames in the arms of a woman who had run toward other survivors and asked them to help the other victims. That same child, the mystery woman said, had neither a first name, nor a family name. And since the boy seemed very intrigued by the brilliance of the fire that reflected like stars in his eyes, the town had opted to name him "Nelson St★", at the suggestion of the woman who had carried him out of the flames.

But why the name Nelson? Was it perhaps to fit the boy's background, or his future, instead? Nelson means "the son of Neal" (Neil . . .), a name which in turn means Champion! A "champion from the stars?" (As the writer York Aurel once said: "The key to the coffer of your golden relics should open the treasures of your life!") And if you ask: "Well, what's in a name, anyway?" the answer is: "Just ask history!" Also, as was mentioned earlier, that this young boy had been given to a mature couple for care. The "mystery woman" had added, besides, that the elementary school records had been sent to an educational institution named The First High School, a private school that had accepted the child, and that for some obscure reason such records were never returned to the town's archives. . . . Some reporters wanted to dig deeper into Nelson's youthful education during the time he was at the different schools he attended, but every inquiry had been met by a complete silence and a total lack of information—in the name of national security. What's even more interesting is that the last educational institution Nelson attended, had referred these inquiring reporters to something calling itself the Office of Communications for the Federally Funded Institutions of Higher Learning.

No wonder! A bogus bureau of which nobody knew the existence, though an office space had actually been listed and some names had been assigned to fill in the titles of Director, of Treasurer, and of Records Manager.

Yes—and who were they? People who could never be traced! An affidavit indicating that Nelson had been under the tutelage of several foster families and that he had "gone away, out of the region," was the only document remaining as a record of his existence. Although the last high school he had attended probably furnished the best and the most complete background about him, their records simply said that Nelson was "good at learning and in sports."

What had greatly dismayed the investigators, however, was the fact that when they decided to question again that same woman who had given them so much information, she could not be found anywhere, and no one knew where to find her. Police officials, ecclesiastic and civic leaders testified that that woman had come to their town only a couple of months before, with the purpose of studying the population in that section of the country, a sort of census taker, who had founded an archive containing records showing the town's and the peoples' background from twenty-five years before the fire, and for almost twenty-five more years after the fire had happened. It also became apparent that her recent sudden departure had also been a puzzle for all of them, mainly since the records that she had kept had mysteriously disappeared along with her. Everyone swore that no one knew who this woman really was, or to have ever seen her before! That her only legacy was what she had given the town's judge before disappearing—a notebook, a mysterious logbook, that had formed part of the school principal's private records at the elementary school that had been burnt down forty-five years before. A logbook containing an entry indicating that a woman of about thirty-seven years of age, who had come to town only a couple of days earlier, and who had been trained in nursing as well as pedagogy, was in reality a teacher. In fact, she was the same teacher that the town had hired weeks before she had arrived, though still pending approval by municipal and ecclesiastical authorities.

The logbook did not specify her name or the school subject she was supposed to teach, though—just an entry indicating she had finally arrived in town, plus the date and the time of the meeting that had taken place in school. Speculation about the logbook indicated, however, that such entry date was the exact day when the town had become a living hell. And the hour? Perhaps the same time at which the woman had been walking away from school, on her way home after that meeting. . . . So, the results of the investigation were inconclusive. Those who had testified about knowing Nelson today, or to have known him then, were confused now. Nelson's genealogical background was, for those reasons, never fully understood. And any facts of his existence before the fire never revealed. Was he the "man without a name?" Was he indeed "a man"—in the human sense of the word? Hypothetically speaking, Nelson's life had, to intents and purposes, begun at the human age of forty-six. And, furthermore, since any questions concerning his married life, and the lives of his family's members, were dismissed as too painful to even be mentioned!, Nelson, therefore, remained not only a total mystery, but the subject of everyone's constant investigation.

4

To aggravate the circumstances, as if Nelson did not have enough problems already, a very serious accident put in jeopardy his ability to compete, with possible disastrous consequences for his entry into the Olympics. At about the same time of this investigation, cyclists from many parts of the country had congregated for one of the regional championship competitions. Nelson did not want to let this opportunity to demonstrate his ability pass him by. Three towns were connected by the route that the three-day event would follow.

This route had been chosen as the training ground for the preliminary selection of Olympic contenders. Important for the athletes as a point maker for the final selection, it had no special attraction for the fans outside the route's lines. Although it was not a difficult competition for the cyclists, it was nevertheless a dangerous one, having a tricky terrain where extreme caution had to be observed in order to stay on . . . and to be able to finish. Why was this road selected, anyway? Perhaps the fact that it contained all types of terrain that must be included in any bicycle competition. Steep mountain roads, flat surface tracts and precipitous slopes made the three day race challenging enough for any professional cyclist hoping to achieve a "mini-tour" triumph.

Although most of the cyclists knew the road well, many were skeptical about certain areas and did not like the overall condition of its surface. A specific section was still dirt, with loose gravel filling in the holes that had been opened by the rains and by the heavy traffic of large vehicles fully loaded with repair and construction equipment. Worst of all, about one-fifth of a mile of that same sector of the road was under constant repair and consequently in extremely bad shape. For months there had been interruptions in the daily traffic routine. Accidents were a constant occurrence, and even closings for days at a time, in both directions, had become a nuisance to travelers. The epicenter of the problem was a steep declivity going deeply toward the middle of the mountain. At the end of that slope, an almost impossible "U" turn had to be negotiated. Any cyclist descending at high speed would be unable to control the bike and most certainly would fall.

A small creek cascaded from the middle of the mountain. Its waters went under a short and narrow bridge that had been built on a temporary basis, and which was merely a wooden platform, with no safety rails on either side. This bridge, which formed the center of the "U" turn, was constantly in repair because of damage produced by the waters flooding several hundred feet on both sides of the road. Beneath the bridge the strength of the waters had already opened a ravine, and on both sides of the mountain, divided as the two sections of a half-way open book, the stream had caved in, dropping its waters into what had already become an abyss. The Devil's Turn was the name given by the local people to this trouble spot.

Approximately two hours into the competition, a peloton composed of about sixteen cyclists, one of them Nelson St★, arrived at that section of the route. They formed position number three following a group of four, which occupied the second place, after an escapee, solitary, number one cyclist.

Among those sixteen competitors from group three were several who had never traveled this road before. Anxious to escalate the attack on group number two, and oblivious to the danger ahead, three cyclists, each from a different team, decided to use the road's declivity to accelerate the pace. Unfortunately they did not realize, until too late, that the surface was very slippery. And it never occurred to them, either, that to be able to make the "U" turn, under such conditions, they would have to slow down, creating chaos for the rest of the cyclists who, undoubtedly, would have increased their speed to try to catch up with them.

As expected, in the middle of the descent, the three escapees suddenly discovered their fatal mistake, but still did not fully comprehend its grave consequences. Trying to avoid crashing against the opposite side of the mountain, at an uncontrolled speed, all three pressed their bikes' brakes at unison. *Holy tandem!!!* Their sudden freeze in action catapulted the riders behind them onto the rear of their bicycles, hitting cyclist against cyclist, with the speed and the impact of a rolling stone.

Bikes were entangled, bodies were mangled, bones and hopes were shattered; death had left its calling card! When the people in the sponsoring vehicles arrived minutes later, the disaster had already occurred. Among the bloody scraps of bicycle metal, and in the sticky mud on this side of the bridge, lay one of the riders, with a broken back and multiple wounds. By a miracle, he had not fallen on the opposite side of the stream, which formed the open space into the deep precipice created by the creek. His injuries were mortal. Still, he did survive long enough to be able to give his version of the accident. Only five of the sixteen riders were able to continue, not having realized at that moment the magnitude of the situation. The others had wounds too serious. Nelson was prone on the side of the road. A bike's pedal had cut his left leg, making an incision just below the knee, and he was bleeding profusely. But luckily for him, of the first ambulance that arrived at the scene, out came a female nurse who went straight toward him and, after observing the gravity of his injury, she proceeded to apply immediately the needed first aid to his wounded leg. For some reason, there again, Nelson, in spite of his blinding pain (or perhaps seeking consolation under such stressful circumstances), couldn't help gazing deeply into her eyes; and while calmly but very professionally she performed the duties of her job, her piercing eyes looked into Nelson's with a steady but friendly stare at the same time that he was receiving the comforts of her treatment. She made him evoke, momentarily, in fast flashes, the memory of that woman he had previously observed as a ghost superimposed over the pictures of his dear family. He was also reminded of the face that had been observing him during that night when he was climbing the mountain. Even more inexplicable is that her face brought, besides, in subsequent stages, the memory of the devastating fire and of its bright and powerful flames that had fascinated him so much, when he was just a small child. *Was this a coincidence, perhaps?*

After a few minutes, the scene of the cycling accident had been transformed into a battlefield hospital. When the other competitors arrived and learned the horrible truth, they decided not to continue. They mourned their fallen comrade in sports by accompanying his body, Indian file behind his official vehicle, forming a cortege. The not so gravely wounded though were sent in their own accompanying cars to the nearest hospitals.

Nelson's case was probably the worst. His bleeding was too copious to control, and he had to be flown by helicopter to one of the largest and best equipped facilities in the capital city.

The competition was declared "incomplete due to uncontrollable circumstances." However, those who had crossed the finish line were awarded trophies. *(A moment of Olympic altruism filled with spiritual beauty, was lived-on then.*

*... The first competitor at the finish line who, by the way, was to-
tally unaware of the accident, added a sportsmanlike touch by ded-
icating his triumph to the one who had just died. . . .)* The tolling
of the bells of death had damped the souls of the athletes
with the shedding of the blood by the fallen champions.
Still, the Olympic spirit, the heart of sports, was alive and
well!

The second round of the exact same event was scheduled to take place days later. Nelson's wound, with his
abundant loss of blood, made it impossible for him to compete and, consequently, imperative for him to withdraw
from the race. Unfortunately he also had to remain hospital-
ized for a few slow passing and agonizing weeks. His con-
valescence was long, and his return to training was painful.

Although the emotional wounds, still open since his
family had died several months before, were not as visible
as the physical one he had just received on his left knee, they
lasted longer and left scars deeper than skin, *indeed!* During
his long days and nights at the hospital, Nelson suffered
more emotionally than physically. He could not prevent
himself from reminiscing about the circumstances of the accident in which his wife, his boy and his two young daughters had died, and about the days that followed such a
calamitous course of events. His mind wandered constantly
back to the time he had spent at the side of his family members after the accident, reliving those painful hours, and the
vivid details of that horrible disaster. The memory of the agony of his wife and of one of his daughters clinging to life,
had made him forget his own pain and feel instead the one
they had experienced. Nelson blamed himself for their fate,
taking upon himself, once again, the anguish of their lamen-
table situation. And while lying in bed, all alone in the hospital, his excruciating pain was partially relieved while his

mind relived over and over again, as if viewed in a film projector's loop, all the circumstances of that tragedy.

Nelson remembered painfully every word spoken between him and his wife, before she and the children had left the house on that beautiful but tragic morning on the first Sunday of the month of July. He remembered clearly embracing and kissing her and his two daughters (but for some obscure reason that he still cannot comprehend, shaking hands with his son for the very first time instead of embracing him and giving him a paternal kiss, and jokingly, again, saluting the boy in a military manner. *Why?*) He remembered that he had said, also jokingly, that the word *good-bye* seemed more appropriate for a long journey than for a trip to the beach! He also remembered the smiles on their faces while they were happily preparing the food for that day's picnic, and while all three had posed for the camera as models in the swim suits they had bought just days before. And how his boy had asked if it was OK for him to try on the swimming trunks he had given his dad on Father's Day.

"Those pants are too big for you," Nelson had answered. "Don't tell me you are as big as your daddy now, are you?"

"No, Dad, they are so nice looking, I just want to see how they fit, so you can buy me a pair for my birthday too," the boy had said.

To this witticism Nelson had replied: "Oh, sure . . . you can have them, at least for today, son. Go ahead, try them on!"

Then he had added while adopting a bodybuilder stance, flexing his arms to demonstrate his well developed biceps, and holding the air inside of his chest expanded as a balloon while turning toward his wife with a pseudo-conceited smile on his face and an air of masculine supremacy in his words, jokingly: "Of course, he is not going to look as handsome as I will when I finally try them on myself. . . . But," to his son, "try them on anyway."

Also, his wife's retort while shaking her head positively, along with a smile of approval: "Our son is better looking than you are . . . and don't you forget it!"

"You hear that, son?" Nelson had answered.

Yes, indeed. He remembered *everything*! Those images were still very clear in his mind. How painful it was to revive the moments during which all three kids begged him to set aside his writing for the day, so that he could accompany them on that outing. He made promises to them that he would definitely go with them the next time around, . . . promises that he now would never carry out. He remembered the children waving good-bye from the friend's car, until he could no longer see their faces. And later on . . . the worries. Ah! Those sempiternal worries always making him imagine the worst—that something bad was going to happen, and that when it did, he would not be able to be there just when he was needed the most. The phone call from the Police Department, asking him his name and address for no apparent reason, and requesting the names of his wife, his son and of his two daughters, besides the name of the lady driver of the car (as if he had been aware of the situation in advance . . .), and their whereabouts that Sunday in July.

He remembered the eternity of those minutes, between that phone call and the time the police arrived at his apartment to bring the news of the accident, and to ask him to accompany them to the hospital. Yes, he remembered all this and, in certain ways, he even understood it. But there was something, however, Nelson could not put his finger on, and that was the ineluctable fact that only minutes after the time his beloved ones had driven away and out of his sight, he had mentally again "seen" the face of that woman who was by now very familiar, but whose ID did not trigger any recollection. He could swear, however, that the driver of the car that had decimated his lovely family, whose photograph was shown to him by the police, and the ghost woman, had been one and the same!

Were they?

Subconsciously, he knew!

Yet, he did not!

Still, he had asked himself: was the woman in his subconscious the cause of that accident?

There was no answer. That realization had brought Nelson a sort of premonition; a presentiment. But much more! A state of mind he could not comprehend.

Then he endured the ride from his apartment to the police station, not knowing what to expect at his arrival. Add the agony of being told by the police officers that the occupants of the vehicles involved had been injured, and that they had been taken to the nearest medical facilities. In his mind was still vivid the 'look' of the nurse who had answered the police officers' questions, and who gave them the room number, and permission to go up for a short visit.

In Nelson's memory he could see himself again, accompanied by one police officer and by the doctor on duty, entering the section on that floor, where the critical patients were kept separate from everyone else, and where he could clearly see the two beds, where his wife and his oldest daughter were resting still unconscious.

But the most vivid memory of that day, however, is the fact that he could not see—anywhere—either his son or his youngest daughter. Unable to communicate with his wife or his older daughter, and urged by the doctor to leave the room, he could only mutter the questions: "Where is she? Where is he?" And when the doctor's and the police officer's exchange of looks had sufficed as an answer, Nelson recalled, brokenhearted, that he had sat in the waiting room for a few long minutes, and forgetting himself and his surroundings, he had finally cried as if he were a child. . . .

He could not forget either when moments later, the doctor, still in the company of one police officer, a sergeant, had brought him a glass of water, and had asked him to go with them downstairs. . . . "Just by thinking about it, I get goose bumps!" he had told a friend later. Yes! The pain he felt at seeing the still bodies of his beloved son and gorgeous baby daughter, promptly made him forget everything else he had seen that day. Perhaps the freezing temperature inside that room had kept his blood from boiling and his heart from collapsing, since his mind had already been melted by the events of that tragic day. . . .

He also remembered thinking that returning alone to his empty apartment wouldn't have made absolutely any sense at all. So, after making a few telephone calls to relatives of his wife, and to some of his old time friends, he then had decided to stay in the hospital, at the bedside of his beloved family.

But then he had been quickly and painfully informed by further news that both his wife and his older daughter had also passed away! *Requiem æternam dona eis Domine, lux perpetua luceat eis. Requiescant in pace! . . ."*

One thing Nelson could not remember—how did he get back home? Walking out of the hospital, he paced the streets for hours without any sense of direction. The feelings he had during that time, and whatever thoughts came to his mind, could not ever again be recollected. He did recall, however, entering a pub, ordering a pint of the strongest black beer they served along with a bottle of cognac, and then placing himself at a table in the darkest corner of the tavern. And that for a while, he forgot his own existence and the existence of the world around him. . . .

"Hey, buddy. Are you OK?" were the words of the bartender, shouting across the room from behind the counter, politely asking that he "take it easy" with the drinking. But Nelson did recall that it was after midnight when a prolonged and very strong knocking at his door, combined with the incessant ringing of the doorbell, brought him back to reality. He was in his apartment and one of the friends whom he had called earlier, had finally received his message, and had been tracking him down. Dr. Rœderick Blake had rushed over to express his condolences, and to offer help in arranging the burial procedures. Again, Nelson also recalled that from the moment when he had been brought back to reality by his friend's knocking at the door (yes, from that moment on, and until after the burial ceremonies), and the gathering at the cemetery, his mind had been totally empty. The persons who attended the services; the funeral cortege; the site of the graves; the words spoken; all were a blank in his mind. Although, back at his apartment a few days later everything *seemed* the same, he could not get used to the routine of being alone at the end of the day's work. The thought of his loneliness, produced by the absence of everyone in his family, that family he had practically abandoned many years before when he had moved out of the house and had gone to live by himself (during which time he had indulged in a love affair with Stewardess, the gorgeous girl next door, before his space mission assignment . . .), sank ever more deeply, into his heart, and kept on bringing back the painful memories of the tragedy.

That's when Nelson had decided to make a complete change of environment by accepting employment as the regional manager of the Film to Tape Transfer Operations and Distribution, located at the International Offices headquarters. Coming from an important government position where he had autonomy to dictate his desires for many years, to a managerial job with a comparatively small size corporation, in a quiet town, brought nevertheless some welcome changes in the life of Nelson St★, indeed.

His new superiors gave him the opportunity to dedicate more time to pursue his writing and to become proficient in all his sports. In spite of the fact that those changes did help emotionally, they were not as stimulating as he had thought they would be. His pervading loneliness, emphasized by the simplicity of his new living conditions, seemed to have accentuated the feeling that nothing on Earth could change him now. However, with more time for extracurricular activities, he concentrated mainly on writing his biography. And from time to time he dedicated extra hours of his self-imposed training routines to try to climb the mountain that served as a background for that town. This butte had challenged him from the beginning—not only because he wasn't physically fit, but mostly because of the fact that it was seen by Nelson as a formidable emotional obstacle. Recurring images of the devastating flames engulfing him, and of the vision of the ghost woman, superimposed like a three-dimensional sign over that mountain, had also been brought back.

So, Nelson became consumed by the idea of climbing it, successfully, as the only solution to his despairing state of mind. Unfortunately, he had failed every single time he had attempted its conquest.

Nelson remembered having read somewhere that an athlete's toughest competition is himself! Well—for Nelson St★ the conquest of that mountain would be the conquest of himself; and his triumph over it sooner or later would give him the victory he needed to elevate his mind and spirit to the highest degree, thus to redeem himself from past failures.

His motto then became "Conquer Thyself!..." The worst part of it all was the fact that he could not help wishing to be able to improve conditions relevant to his future athletic career and he tortured himself at realizing that he had been unable to do anything to remedy his family's situation at the time of that sinister event. He felt now, as he had then, totally impotent. And his physical pain was allowing him no rest, serving as a constant reminder of the troubles and tribulations of his recent past. But—time heals everything....

Weeks flew by. The widely publicized case of the cyclists' accident, and especially of Nelson's hospitalization, had long faded away. And in a reversal of public opinion, at the time of his release from the hospital, the media, for no apparent reason, had become totally indifferent, sometimes even deprecatory. Nelson could not really understand why his unfortunate injury had become the departing point that would detract from his possibilities of Olympic triumph. To the media Nelson was no longer the promising athlete who could, perhaps someday, become a new decathlon champion; they seemed to have nothing constructive to offer at this time. As a matter of fact, Nelson was now just an almost fifty-year-old individual who was trying to compete against well-trained twenty-year-olds, for his own fame, glory and fortune. Some newspaper editorial comments even advised him not to waste his remaining energy on an impractical mirage. Surely he could save the Olympic authorities' time and money, and himself, some embarrassment, by simply "forgetting" to compete!

But knowing that such ill advice could only come from the frail mentalities of egotistic persons in the business whose profits were at stake, Nelson instead dedicated himself with renewed vigor and devotion to recoup the lost time, and to prove to himself, and to those mediocre individuals with the incapacity for ideals, that he could still become an Olympic winner!

His new adversaries, however, seemed determined to deny him his own chance. The better an athlete he became during training, and the higher he qualified, either when competing or simply when testing himself before a competition, the more verbal and written abuse he had to endure. The fact that he was excellent at what he did, aroused even more suspicion. His athletic abilities, improved day by day with an incredible efficiency, created doubts about his personal and professional integrity. Not having ruled him out of the Olympics then, tests were soon performed not just to find out the truth about this extraordinary individual whose advanced age seemed to defy all odds, and whose prowess had no precedent in the annals of sports. *No.* These tests were designated for the sole purpose of finding evidence to incriminate him, since he could not be condemned beforehand. Fortunately, the truth is only one. No question about it!

The results of the medical tests performed on him only proved that Nelson had a very unusual ability to assimilate food, and to retain large amounts of nutrients. His body appeared to possess a very rare and quite unique functional digestive system, not physically different, however, from that of any other athlete, whose way of releasing its energy reserves was on a kind of "time lapse" manner, not seen by the medical profession until now. (A new "Gordian knot" for the scientific mind to ponder, and to find a replica among the rest of humanity.)

Although Nelson had been exempted from competing in the official eliminatory tests since he was the only representative of "his world," he nevertheless went through the process in every competition required, in order to qualify against the best athletes already pre-selected. However, his extraordinary energy and superior muscular capacity served mainly to arouse suspicion, furnishing those mediocre mentalities and vicious characters the opportunity to pass judgment against him. Fortunately, as is well known, time heals everything, and the mentality of the masses sways with the strongest opinion.

So, in spite of these ups and downs, expectations about Nelson's performance in the coming Olympics grew higher, along with a renewed vote of confidence from the fans. After getting tired of the charade being played by some members of the media obviously influenced by private interests, these fans had once again changed their minds and were now demonstrating their support. They were letting Nelson know in more than one way that their admiration for him was still alive and well and that their renewed way of thinking was going to give him the emotional push needed to carry him all the way to total victory.

Coincidentally, one of Nelson's most celebrated action photographs was published in some widely distributed newspapers. The caption under it simply read: NELSON ST★, THE DECAMPION; ATHLETE OF THE CENTURY! Nelson was never sure if the intention had been to mock his efforts and sacrifices, and if the wording of the article about him had tried to make him a subject of ridicule. "For a person his age," said the newspaper, "everything should be considered a goal achieved, since at his gracious age we all have already done our best. It will be, nevertheless, an outstanding triumph for this extraordinary athlete to at least reach the eliminatory stage. In that manner, we can say that his efforts and hopes were not in vain."

But (and isn't there always a but) as the saying goes: "Things usually turn out for the best." Nelson's picture and the accompanying caption caught the eye of some VIPs from the private sector who were willing to help; thus bringing his court case to a speedy solution. In addition, among the members of the press who had followed closely the minutes of the proceedings, there was a young, extraordinarily attractive journalist, looking for her first internationally reaching assignment. This young woman's interest in Nelson was not merely journalistic. From the very first moment she laid eyes on his picture, her attraction for him, renewed and expanded by special news reports, was such that she had actually requested from her newspaper's chief editor, as a special duty, to cover Nelson's future participation in the Olympics and, specifically, his training at this time.

5

Up to this point Nelson did not have enough time or means to be able to dedicate himself fully to the promotion of his athletic endeavors. However, a generous severance pay for a lifetime of work with the federal government, and his pension fund savings, plus a thirty-three-million-dollar winning bonanza from the state's lottery, provided him with enough economic solvency to allow him to use his time and energies at full capacity, pursuing the dream of his life. To paraphrase an old proverb: "There's a time for everything and everything comes at the right time."

Not really searching for fame, nor interested in obtaining fortune per se (two things in life that can always be attained by other means), but as a way to achieve the triumph in sports that he had always dreamt about, Nelson did not stop where most people usually do. On the contrary, he not only took every chance he could at winning by buying every lottery ticket he could afford within reason, for prizes large enough to satisfy every need; but he traveled often and extensively at his own expense, in order to grab every possibility, no matter how remote, believing that one day, his lucky moment of fortune would finally arrive. From state to state, from city to city, he searched for that lucky chance. Nelson never really lacked absolutely anything. The U.S. government had provided for the smallest detail, and had fulfilled every need for himself, and for his family. Having gone through life without the things everybody else considered luxurious, and not having the luck he believed should have been his just by right of birth, he was certain that by trying harder and often he would one day finally beat the odds, and obtain his wish. And with luck bringing in the economic means, fame would eventually come along as a corollary.

Be it understood that though Nelson did not spare any means when the circumstances were favorable, he did not waste any in futile pursuit either. He took only the risks that were within his range and those he considered appropriate, economically and otherwise. Though not a gambler in the true sense of the word, Nelson enjoyed himself primarily dreaming about riches and travels, for his own amusement. Traveling for the purpose of recreation while visiting new locations in different states constituted an enjoyment of life for him, and at the same time served his purposes by giving him the chance to buy the lottery tickets he wanted. Of course, not every trip was taken just for the purpose of obtaining those possible winning tickets. No; some tickets were bought only while on a pleasure outing (surely not the province of a compulsive gambler) but merely as a complement to the joy of the trip, keeping in mind, besides, the possibility of reimbursement for the trip itself. It was still gambling, you say? But, doesn't everyone take a chance in life every day? A day dreamer, yes; but one, it must be said, with a sense of responsibility toward himself. Never going above or beyond his economic capacity, Nelson did sometimes spend more than he should have, based on his blind trust on his own intuition, which had brought him perhaps a little farther than his own possibilities. But his moral character and his sense of righteousness never allowed Nelson to be dominated by a desire for money and luxury. He refused to be diverted from what he considered to be his normal behavior. (And what is the meaning of "normal" anyway? In other words, never against the morally established principles.) Was Nelson merely subconsciously denying his own compulsion? Gambling, of course, is wrong, according to moralists—no matter how you excuse it. But even if Nelson was indeed denying it, no moralist would have been able to find a better plot in which to plant his moral seeds. Still, even though Nelson knew and understood the moral implication concerning gambling, he would not allow extreme restrictive thinking to stand in his way either. "Life is too precious for one to destroy the small pleasures it provides," Nelson believed—(though he still also believed abstention is the best precaution against vicious extremes). However, Nelson's independent way of thinking would not have allowed the development of such seeds of morality and/or prudence. Nevertheless, to each his own! But since the government gives itself the right to impose upon its citizens not only laws against gambling but the rules to break those same laws when it regulates their use and when it levies a tax as the authorization for the breaking of the law to be acceptable, then who is to say that it is wrong? Attached to the same principles of right and wrong, these laws are then called "legal ways . . ."—as long as the government is compensated for it! "To Caesar what belongs to Caesar." There are plenty of people who take it upon themselves to try to convince the world that almost everything one does today is morally wrong. Most of them end their public dissertation by telling you that for a dollar he or she will save you from damnation. Protected by our system of laws, these moralists gamble their way to your pocket through the intricate crevices of your heart and mind.

"Gambling," per se, does not necessarily include only those who are feebleminded, of course. What's even worse is the fact that those who preach morality, turn around and commit the same immoral acts they preach against.

Nelson thought the state's lotteries were one of the legally acceptable ways to obtain his riches, and to achieve his dreams. While the saying: "If you think you are going to win . . . don't bet on it . . ." has proved true for some skeptics,

Nelson's own adage: "If you don't expect to win . . . you have already lost . . ." kept him going strong, playing lotteries in all the states where they were obtainable, and even from some international agencies, when the stakes were good.

Nelson never really condoned gambling. Of course, not! What's more, he always told his acquaintances (those who knew he played the lottery for instance), that if they ever did gamble, they should do it in a conscientious manner. And, guess what? By doing just that himself, he was lucky enough to finally achieve the economic independence that allowed him to obtain the necessary resources to bring to realization what he had wanted to do all his life. That included, of course, the means for him to practice some special sports under the appropriate professional guidance. And besides satisfying himself, he now possessed the fiscal ability to realistically enter the Olympic Games competition. To be a participant (but hopefully a winner) in the Olympic decathlon! Wasn't he lucky? (By the way, are the Olympic Games a gamble?)

The realization of his dream was becoming now a possibility—under the auspices of those special beings he had met, he was sure. *Or was it the influence of his lucky star?* What a gamble it was!

For many years Nelson lost almost every single penny he gambled. Only rarely was the money he invested in lottery tickets (and the expenses he incurred while traveling to buy them) fully reimbursed. But he never lost faith in his luck, or in the possibility of actually winning one lottery large enough to fulfill his wishes. And despite his constant failures, he kept on trying. One lesson, perhaps, in perseverance, although one without the moral connotation in this instance! For some people this way of thinking might indicate a lack of understanding of facts, and/or a disregard for moral behavior, and/or a total absence of mind, neither of which allows the bettor to differentiate between reality and fantasy; but for most again, it is just a way of poking at Lady Luck while enjoying the suspense, and at the same time having fun. "The good or bad of it, depends on the individual," Nelson always said. "No harm done, really, if you play conscientiously!" (Of course, you might add, just like the government and the religious preachers, Nelson committed the sin and gave himself the absolution!)

One day finally he had a premonition. While on a pleasure weekend trip to visit friends who had bought a brand new house on an isolated neighborhood in the outskirts of a small town, in one of the adjacent states, Nelson saw an ad about that state's lottery, announcing the amount of the jackpot for the week's drawing. Strange as it might sound, he was immediately convinced that this prize was exactly what he was going to win. Under the pretext that he was going to "look around the area" before going to the friends' house, he went into the town and bought some lottery tickets. At home again a couple of days later while notating the expenses of the trip, he remembered he had invested a few dollars in that special drawing, and proceeded to check the results. You can not believe the astonishment of Nelson St★ when he heard the recorded message with the winning numbers, and realized that one of his tickets matched exactly the ones that had been selected as the winner! Making an immediate telephone call to the Lottery Regional Office, an official corroborated his findings and gave him instructions on how to proceed to claim this extraordinary monetary prize.

Unable to sleep while his heart was so overwhelmed with emotions beyond his control, Nelson did not go to work the next day. Instead, he went by train to the Regional Lottery Claim Center in that state's capital, and registered his lucky ticket. A receptionist took him into a large and comfortable office where he was met first by a secretary whose energetic approach left a great impression on Nelson. A sweet, rotund individual with an extraordinarily powerful speech pattern, an impeccable British accent and a delightful tone of voice that was simply mesmerizing. The way she expressed herself was as fluent as a waterfall and with such clarity and precision that William Shakespeare himself would have been very proud of her. She had a very attractive face "adorned" by a timid mustache that gave her a kind of distinguished look, disfigured, unfortunately, by a non-lit cigar "jumping" constantly from side to side in her mouth. Her eyes, two round big black eyes, kept Nelson staring at hers while her voice pierced the mental cavity of his brain. She also proceeded to help him fill out some required forms, and to give Nelson the final figures of the transaction.

A few minutes later two gentlemen entered that office and introduced themselves. One was the Commissioner for that State's Lottery, and the other the State's Lottery Treasurer. . . . After being congratulated, Nelson identified himself at their request. The secretary had now finished filling in the details on the documents that made Nelson the sole possessor of the contract (and the sole owner of a very large fortune). Everyone present signed it, and then hands were shaken all around. An invitation for lunch was followed by the request to Nelson that he pose for a couple of photographs for the official press release. However, no press conference was called; it was replaced instead by a short article, using a pseudonym, in order to avoid unnecessary publicity for him.

Nelson then was driven in a luxurious limousine to a prearranged location, a restaurant where lottery winners were the usual guests of honor. He was plied with caviar, champagne, flowers and the usual congratulatory kisses from some beautiful girls, part of the entourage, making the occasion a little more special for the new multimillionaire. The rest of the afternoon was spent sightseeing in their company.

When night came, dinner was in order. Still accompanied by some of the people he had met earlier, Nelson went to a very chic continental restaurant where he enjoyed the wines and the food of his pleasure. Inviting these new "friends," Nelson St ★ now truly felt himself to be a millionaire. "Have you ever heard what is said about luck?" asked Nelson expansively of his companions, savoring the situation.

Before anyone could define the word or remember the quotation (that it comes down as a downpour), luck proved that it was his lady that night. Luck proved itself that day. On his trip to the casino, following dinner that evening, every chance he took at the slot machines was abundantly remunerated. Feeling generous, as well as lucky, his generosity spilled all over to those gorgeous girls who were still keeping him company. Their personal gratitude was then extended well beyond the professional courtesies for which they had been initially engaged . . . but only after having been released from their duty. A box of the house's best cigars, and a good sized bottle of the best cognac, went also to the individual Nelson had considered the "largest brain walking around!"

The next day, Nelson went to the bank to deposit his first installment check. And with a rare feeling in his heart (that unusual feeling he had not experienced since his trek to space, a feeling indicative of a better and of a special time to come), which became a feeling of power, that made him imagine that not only was the world his own, but that he was a giant of such magnitude that he would be able now to even "play soccer," in a manner of speaking, with the spheric (as the soccer ball is commonly called in some parts of the world) of planet Earth, and with the globes of the rest of the worlds in our solar system, in the open "fields" of the Milky Way galaxy, he returned to work. Feeling that power, he went back to his office . . .

Days later, after having completed his plans for entering the Olympics as a contestant, Nelson terminated his professional relationship with a letter to his recently found employers. (Under the given circumstances it might be said that no one had a better excuse, ever, for retiring early from an office job.) Nelson's gambling had finally paid off. Lucky . . . or was he?

6

After cruising through the main streets of Nelson's town, the driver of an elegant, late model convertible, stopped in front of a building where the offices of the town's main newspaper were located. A woman stepped out of the car, and went inside. Minutes later, she came out and walked back to her vehicle; then she drove around the park and came to a stop on the side of the sheriff's car, that was parked in the middle of an intersection as if to prevent traffic from going in any direction. The woman, from her vehicle, called the sheriff to attention by waving at him, after having blown the horn a couple of times. The sheriff then approached the driver's side of the car. The woman's questions, after proper identification had been established, were answered while he signaled in which direction to go.

Thanking the sheriff with a kind of military hand salute gesture, the woman took off, getting lost in the outskirts. A quarter of an hour later, she was parked on a little hill on the side of the road, standing inside of her car, semi-squatting behind the car's steering wheel. Leaning with both arms behind her to support herself against the driver's seat, she observed for a few minutes the mountainous terrain in front of her, trying to find the exact location where she was supposed to meet Nelson St★.

A few minutes later, and simultaneously, while Nelson was preparing to escalate a steep hill on the open dirt road he knew so well, this woman was driving at high speed approaching an intersection where she had been told she would be able to find him. Concentrating on his bike, Nelson was totally unaware of her coming. He was at a section of the road authorized by the traffic department, which he had selected specifically for his daily practice, mainly because of its hard terrain and unusual configuration.

Suddenly, without any warning and out of nowhere, Nelson's bike was struck by the woman's car reckless invasion of his side of the road. The car's fender lightly tapped the rear tire of Nelson's bike, sending him flying into a ditch. ("It was an accident," she said afterward, but it really appeared to be an intentionally planned act, for the purpose of gaining his attention.) For his good fortune however, the trench was not too deep. Instead, it was filled with soft mud and covered with high, thick layers of grass and short bushes.

Out of the car, a concerned and worried person came running to help Nelson out of his predicament.

Nelson's body, due to the height of the shrubs, seemed to have sunk only half way into the ditch. But he was wet and covered with dirt. His face looked like a plastic mask and his eyes were blinded with mud. He was indeed upset but, fortunately, not hurt. Lying in the ditch, practically buried alive among the thick bushes, he did not move for a while.

When the woman driver finally came close to him near the long and narrow trench on the side of the road, Nelson could not even see her face. Apologizing repeatedly for the inconvenience she had caused him, and admitting her guilt in the distressful incident, she could not, however, pass up such a set of career-enhancing circumstances.

"Don't move! Please, don't move," were the first words she spoke directly to Nelson, among her excuses and apologies, while he was still "buried" in that trench. Without wasting any time she went back to her car and, after grabbing her camera, she returned to the scene of the accident and took several snapshots of Nelson still lying on the ground. Although Nelson's reaction to her moves was calm, deeply inside he was about to explode. By the time Nelson had pulled himself together and finally cleaned his face, her apologies had subsided, and laughter, nervous laughter had replaced her remorse. A few moments of tense silence followed the sound of her voice.

Nelson then got up. Between straightening out his bike, and removing mud from the rest of his body, he mumbled some curses, that caught her by surprise.

"I am truly sorry," she said once again, in an insincere tone of voice that carried no comfort to Nelson.

Looking at her now with a measuring eye, Nelson said drastically: "It's fine, it's fine! I just can't afford to repeat what happened some time ago. . . . But I feel OK!" Unable to repair his bike, however, Nelson threw it aside. He then looked for a soft spot on the ground and silently lay down. Quietly, she approached him while snapping some extra photographs.

"Who the heck are you? And what are you doing in this neck of the woods?" snarled Nelson.

After the lady had joined him sitting on the grass, they introduced themselves. At the sound of his voice and at the mention of his name, she became ecstatic! His name, obviously, evoked memories from the past, and especially from the last few months—during which time she had been following very closely the ups and downs of Nelson's aspiring Olympic career.

"My name is Cynthia. I am a journalist and, believe it or not, I was looking for you. The chief editor of the town's newspaper, and the sheriff himself told me that you usually train around here at this time of the day," responded Cynthia.

"And now that you have found me, what can I do for you?" replied Nelson.

"Before I tell you, I need to know that you are OK; I then need to ask you for a favor . . ." said Cynthia.

"What? Are you serious? My goodness!" exclaimed Nelson, shaking his head with a gesture of incredulity. Then, reacting to his own words, he tried to apologize with his answer: "Well, I don't think there are any broken bones . . . if that's what you mean," added Nelson while examining his body for possible injuries.

"You see," continued Cynthia, "I know who you are. I have been observing you during your training schedules for quite a while—and I've seen you in competitions for as long as you have been entering them and participating. And as you can deduce, I am very interested in your professional success." Then, as coquettishly as she could, and while staring at him with tremendous curiosity as if trying to learn every feature of his face in spite of his muddy mask, "Oh, you are so handsome! And you look so cute all covered with dirt!" added she in a longing and complaisant kind of voice.

"As a matter of fact, besides my very serious interest in your professional life, I like you also as a man, something I take very personally . . ." continued Cynthia, a little bit embarrassed. "Please forgive me, but I had to tell you that!" she finished.

"I am flattered," answered Nelson. "It is refreshing to know that at my age, I still possess some appeal for beautiful women such as yourself." Then he added: "What is the favor?"

"Well," Cynthia began, "I would like to have an exclusive on all the news about you, so that I might be able to build a portfolio with all the information, old and new, about your life, and about your new career as an athlete and a participant in the Olympics."

Then she said: "I know it is also my own career I am trying to advance, but . . ."

"I know, I know, I know . . . and I understand," interrupted Nelson. "In fact," he added then in a very gallant way, "I am glad you said that because it means that you and I will have to be very close until the very last moment of the Closing Ceremonies!" Stunned by his answer in spite of the fact that she did not really understand the full meaning of his last words, Cynthia, showing some pleasure, invited him to bring his badly bent bike to her car. And both then drove away. . . .

Cynthia was a twenty-seven-year young filly, five feet ten inches tall; slender, beautifully built, with elegant red hair, green eyes, much "get-up-and-go"; a distingué woman who, by her own account, had given up a promising athletic career to accept a journalism scholarship from one of the nation's news organizations. Having completed her schooling with the highest possible degree, and after receiving honors for her work in different areas of her career, she still preferred the domain of the down-to-Earth reporter, and had refused several other lucrative positions in the field, on her way up. However, she was constantly on the look-out for the next opportunity to jump ever higher on the ladder of success (strictly as a journalist), simply out of love for her profession. Although she really was a professional in every sense of the word, and her intentions were mainly to serve Nelson's athletic needs, in this particular instance she also felt, personally, deeply attracted toward him. By telling Nelson privately, "Though I am willing to sacrifice part of my personal life in order to achieve my professional goals," she had expressed to him what was the real truth as she felt it in her libidinous heart. At least, she *was* truthful, and to the point.

Looking at her beauty as a woman—so feminine, so sweet, so attractive, so delicious looking, and above all so desirable as a female, Nelson, as a man, gladly placed her at the top of the lot in the category of the female of the species. And listening to the way she stipulated her desire for certain conditions that would benefit her personally, as well as her own career, he, understanding well her character, as the athlete in need of help, thought of her at the same time as the true prototype of the business-minded individual. A complete person; no buts about it!

In Cynthia's car, and after a certain rapport had been established recounting moments from his past, and talking as if she had been a long-time friend, Nelson disclosed secrets of his life he had never told anyone else before—events which had taken place during the years he was growing up in or near the town where he supposedly had been born, just a couple of years after the first road had been built. And more recently, after cars, buses, trucks, etc., had been used for public transportation for the very first time, to and from that regional center. And more specifically, recollections from some of the different localities where he had visited school friends, or to spend time with some of the relatives of the current foster parents, mainly during those three, hot, long summer months, in the middle of the year. And of course also during the winter vacation days, in places located in and around the neighboring towns of that same region.

With total naiveté, Nelson went on: "You know, before I was twelve years old, my family lived in a small town where the average temperature was ninety-two degrees Fahrenheit. I mean it was really hot, however pleasantly dry! As I remember it, this small town was a very nice place located in between two rivers flowing south to north, one on the east, and the other on the west side; the rivers engulfed the town like a cocoon around its adjacent fields. Two clean, sweet water, powerful streams, cascading down from the mountains. Two life-giving, large-size creeks, with deep ponds where my friends from school and I used to go swimming and fishing.

"Funny," continued Nelson after a short pause to reflect, "I don't know why I always think of that location with an allegory like that."

"Like what?" said Cynthia.

"Surrounded . . . as a cocoon around a . . . ah . . ." asserted Nelson pensively. "Perhaps because my mother taught me about these beautiful insects" he continued, "like caterpillars, silkworms, centipedes, and spiders, etc., some of which become gorgeous butterflies; those colorful insects more delicate than rose petals though stronger than ethereal snowflakes, telling me never to destroy them or their private habitats; to always admire them instead in their own environment, and to understand that they are on Earth, just like humans are, for a very special reason."

"Your mother used to tell you those things when you were a child?" asked Cynthia. "And did she always put it just that way: 'like humans are,' or did she ever say: like *we* humans are?"

Looking at her suspiciously, Nelson said: "What are you implying, Cynthia?" And after another pause, he answered her first question but ignored the last two. "Yes, often," replied Nelson. And as if nothing had happened, "You know," he continued, "I remember that town as a paradise on Earth, with colorfully painted houses, some with roofs made of straw, giving the impression of being rustic, but looking very attractive and even elegant instead; and very modern inside. Their backyards were planted, sowed with an unbelievable variety of vegetables. Some backyards were made into orchards containing the sweetest tropical fruit trees, and many exclusively with cacao trees—a paradise of green trees permanently abounding with ripe fruit. And the town's plaza, the park, magnificent as a garden, exuberant with different types of exotic plants always bent over with an assortment of flowers, every time of the year I went there. Oh, and a beautiful water fountain in the center. By the way, this fountain was built in a hexagonal form with three layers or grades, like three pools, one on top of the other, the lowest being the largest, probably fifty feet in circumference, and the top the smallest one, resembling those candy dishes or cake holders that look like three floor towers. From each of the pool's surrounding walls and floors, which were built with tiles of different colors, slabs of glazed pottery that reflected light, the water sprang very high at certain intervals. And with the lights flashing also in several colors against the water jets, they made the fountain a technicolor center of attraction and a recreational area for kids of all ages to watch and to admire at certain times of the night. . . . Unfortunately, I also remember my mother quoting a Spanish-speaking priest who had come on a missionary visit to the Indian reservation located nearby, as saying in Spanish that there was no *sociedad* in that place, only *suciedad*, meaning that the moral situation was, to say the least, devastating! And that that decadent situation was perhaps, besides, the reason why you could not associate with anyone, or have any friends, except only from a small circle composed of half a dozen prominent families, the official employees from the government, and the elementary and high school teachers, who usually were from out of town. Maybe that's why I only stayed there for short periods every time. . . . However," insisted Nelson, "I don't see the connection now that I am an adult, between this beautifully kept town and the people in it. It doesn't make any sense. How is it possible to live in a gorgeous place, a paradise as I said before, and to have such moral, social and personal decay? Or is this the way Earth is all about? It may make sense to you, young lady, but I don't get it . . .," continued Nelson, kind of reflecting on the words of that statement.

Cynthia looked at him with an expression of doubt as if aware that his words: "Or is this the way Earth is all about?" were a reflection of his origins!

Then, Nelson continued: "We lived in a good sized house with three bedrooms, a spacious living room and a large kitchen and dining room combination. The rooms were connected internally by a long, open corridor that formed an "L" and that separated the rooms from a patio. In this interior patio was a garden with a fountain right in the center. Also a palm tree without any leaves or fruits because the trunk had been cut down to about one tenth the normal size of the grown palm, and which was located on one of the corners of the patio. The house had also a very beautiful, large-sized backyard, at least three quarters of a block long, full of different fruit trees, palms and flowering plants of several species, that grew naturally and wild."

Nelson stopped here to think, and after a couple of silent minutes during which Cynthia said some words encouraging him to continue with his description, which she really found fascinating, Nelson said: "Making a parenthesis, Cynthia, I am going to tell you something that I really consider a beautiful episode in my life, one which signifies a lot to me, because it puts into perspective my own existence, and illustrates how cruel life can be, even if there is no malicious act to make it so, when life uses fate as bait in its hook!"

Nelson looked at Cynthia's eyes and probed deeply into her soul, to see if his words had any meaning to her. But she did not wink.

"It is the story of two beautiful little loving birds . . . as I used to think, their nest house, and their fate in life."

"Oh," said Cynthia, "that sounds very impressive. What is the story?"

"It was a tragedy, actually, something that made me cry many times afterward," responded Nelson.

"It must be very sad then," replied Cynthia.

"Well," started Nelson. Then he stopped speaking, cutting himself off abruptly.

"When we get together this evening," he said emphatically, "I will tell you the two episodes that are very dear to my heart, because they have something to do with animals. . . . Specifically with horses and birds. OK?"

"That's fine with me," responded Cynthia with a tone of approval though surprised by his sudden change of mood. Then, she added with a warm smile: "Good. It will actually be an excellent topic of conversation during dinner tonight. I'll look forward to it!"

"During the times I was there, in that land between the rivers, in that paradise on Earth, on vacation from schools located in different towns, I used to work a part-time job helping the owner of a grocery store where I made enough money to be able to rent a bicycle late in the afternoons on the days when I didn't work—or early during the evenings of the days I did.

"One day, though, while my parents visited some friends, at about 2 P.M., I rented a bike that I now think was in poor mechanical condition—because when I tried to switch gears while going down the hill, the chain fell off, and the bike had no controls. I was so involved with the problem of the broken chain that I don't think I ever pressed the brake, either for the front, or for the back tire; I kept on going down faster and faster, until I hit the sidewalk at the end of the street, right where it formed the intersection with another one-way, one-lane street, in the manner in which two lines form a 'T'. This impact sent me flying against the

72

wooden frame of a large size, old fashioned window protruding about one foot out of the wall, with its window sill only about three feet above the sidewalk—a window protruding from the wall of a house situated right in the middle section of the crossing lane, directly facing the street where I was riding my bike and against which I hit my head so strongly that I completely passed out. When I woke up, I found myself with my head reclining on the lap of the kind woman who lived in that house. She was sitting on the floor, out on the street, surrounded by a large crowd of neighbors looking on at the scene of the accident, and she was pouring water onto my forehead and massaging my skull. I think I remember that she was also hugging me tenderly, and that she kissed me several times, as if I was a little child in pain."

At this point, Cynthia looked at Nelson and made a deprecative facial gesture of question: "Was she taking the opportunity to satisfy her maternal instincts, or perhaps something else instead . . . huh?"

Nelson simply smiled understandingly, and with a certain kind of egotistic pride at realizing that Cynthia's feelings of jealousy were surfacing.

Then he continued: "When I went home, I did not dare tell my mother about either the accident or the pain I was suffering, but I do remember having a tremendous headache all that evening."

Nelson paused for a moment while shaking his head in a gesture of disbelief; sounding almost apologetic, he said: "God, I almost killed myself by behaving so stupidly!"

Cynthia looked at him with a smile on her face as if fully understanding the feeling. He then continued: "You know, before that bicycle accident happened, something really bad occurred that almost became fatal to me."

Nelson shook his head, as if reminiscing, for an instant. He then started to change the station setting on the car radio and, after instinctively looking first toward the back and then toward the front as if expecting to see someone there, he finally set the radio dial on his favorite classical station instead.

"I was only about six years of age when this episode in my childhood took place." He stopped again, changed position on the seat, and looked at Cynthia's face trying to determine any reaction.

Looking back at him, she said enthusiastically: "Yes! What happened? Tell me all about it. With every teeny-weeny, itty-bitty, mini detail."

Nelson, smiling with satisfaction, added: "Oh ... I thought that perhaps you might be tired of listening to such uninteresting tales."

"Oh, no," replied Cynthia. "Everything that concerns you, concerns me. Remember? I am a reporter with exclusivity on your life's events."

"Well, in that case, I will tell you everything with as much ... ah, how did you put it ... 'teensy-weensy, itsy-bitsy ... disgusting little detail?' as I can remember," responded Nelson with a joking attitude. Then moving around in his seat again, as a hen might move over hatching eggs, he sipped a few large drinks from his water bottle, and continued after a short pause.

". . . This happened, as I said before, when I was about six years old. It was on a Sunday morning, probably before nine. Kind of early for me at that age to be outside the house. I think it was just early enough to attend the religious services. And I believe I was waiting for my mother to take me."

Nelson paused and reflected on.

"We used to live in a large, three-floor family house that had some extra rooms that were sometimes occupied by special guests who visited the town. I believe I told you that my father was the mayor, and my mother was a part-time school teacher—didn't I?

"Well, actually she had founded a kind of secondary school for girls who had already finished the elementary grades. These girls went home to become maids in their families' households once they had finished learning how to write and how to read. So my mother formed a large size group, divided the girls into A.M. and P.M. classes, and offered them extra, more advanced education. My mother taught them, besides the normal academic subjects, some basic business skills so they could also find jobs—either in the same town or in neighboring locations, be solvent enough, and to be able to contribute thereafter to their family's needs.

"For that, my mother was admired by some pupils who brought her presents and made her name famous when they actually became professionals after having finished their advanced education.

"One of them, for example, was an Indian girl who became a lawyer and later on occupied a high position in the state legislature."

"Oh, how beautiful! Helping others intellectually. I praise her," said Cynthia sincerely.

"I thank you, in her name and in mine," added Nelson pausing for a moment. Then, proceeding with new ardor, he continued: "Oh yes—as I was saying, many of the visitors were government officials who came to inspect work being done not only at our place, but at neighboring sites, like on the grounds of the Indian reservation that is still today the property of the Federal Government. Some of the visitors even used to bring me gifts when they returned a second, or even a third time. By the way, I think that the reason for them to return so often was not necessarily because they had to inspect work being done, but because of the intelligent conversation and the good treatment given to them by my parents. Actually, now that I think about it, I believe it was mainly because of the amenities that were included in the price for the spacious room—like excellent food and delicious wines, besides a fantastic garden bath-house. My parents' household was an oasis, practically speaking, in the middle of the desert. No kidding!

"At the back of the building, across from the interior patio where trees and flowers enhanced the atmosphere and cooled the hot air, and on the other side of the wall, secluded from street noise and nosy neighbors, there was a beautiful, very large, very comfortable bath house reminiscent of the Imperial Roman era. It was built around seven wells, each one a small pool of about twelve feet in circumference, in black cement, encircling a very high and elaborately embellished water tower showing figurines of classical angels playing violins, and of beautiful women scantily dressed in transparent veils floating in the air, carrying flowers and fruits, at whose feet semi-naked men built like Hercules begged for attention!

"Each well was separated from the others by high walls but with an open roof to receive the sunlight and its hot rays all day long. And the water? Ah, the water was really a delight! A cascade that covered your body entirely when you went underneath with your back to the source. It had such strength that when the water hit your head, it splashed all over and expanded thinly in every direction, giving the impression it had formed a large hat. Like when you put a huge leaf over your head . . . no, no . . . ah, more like an umbrella. Have you ever done that?"

"No, but I once wore a mariachi hat, if that's what you mean?" replied Cynthia jokingly.

"Ah, c'mon," said he, pausing for a few seconds. "I remember how it also looked at some other times when the sun's position was different," continued Nelson in a reminiscing manner. "It was so beautiful! The water jet, while splashing over your head, and expanding thinly all around, had seemed to have created colorful rainbows by playing matchmaker with the sun's rays."

Here, Nelson paused again. "Well—our house, if I recall properly, was located at a corner of one regular residential street where it met the beginning of a very wide avenue that had been specifically built to connect with a brand new road, a couple of blocks away. This road was at the same time, the access to, and the exit from our town to the other localities in the neighboring counties. I also remember that there were no buildings on the other side of the avenue, across the street from the house. That side had a special wall however, called 'Trincho,' a kind of parapet used to keep pedestrians (as well as vehicular traffic) from making a wrong turn at that point."

Here Nelson stopped momentarily to think about what he was going to say, before he said it.

"Yes, yes, I remember that. Actually, this wall separated the street from a precipice. Yes! At the edge of the street began a slope that went all the way down to a powerful river. This slope was covered with trees with large size canopies, strong trunks and very unusual roots that spread above the ground due to erosion, like the tentacles of an octopus. And due to the inclination of the land, these trees were standing in an almost oblique position in reference to the ground, with plenty of plants and bushes around them. I always thought of that declivity which was covered almost entirely by so many trees, as the 'hanging forest,' after I went down to the river, sliding under the canopies, to go swimming for the first time on a very hot day. On a Wednesday, as I remember. Yeah, it was on a Wednesday afternoon, after school," said Nelson pensively. "Correction! We didn't have school on Wednesday afternoons—school finished at 11 A.M. That's right!" said Nelson now convinced of his excellent memory.

"I was just following a couple of friends who enticed me with their tales of the excitement and pleasure they experienced when diving naked into the lukewarm waters of the river. (At the same time that I was disobeying my parents' orders!) After that day, though, I only committed the same sort of truancy twice, mind you, with the lure of the river's soothing waters as my excuse, and, something else!"

Nelson stopped to reflect. "I even had bad dreams afterwards" he continued. "In my dreams I saw the tall bushes in that slope all put together forming a 'moving lake,' but going down the incline in the way water drops when forming a fall. And I was drowning in those waters in my dream, but with my head above the waters, until I got to the edge of the fall . . . when I woke up! I also saw in another dream those large trees' canopies as the roof of an invisible house," he added reflectively. "The shrubs allowed me to 'walk' on that slope, so to speak, by holding on, either when sliding going down toward the river for a good dip, or when climbing coming back up, after a refreshing plunge in its clear, warm and stimulating waters. Of course—at the bottom of this precipice flowed the beautiful river I mentioned before, with an unusually strong current, the roar of which could be heard as the rumble of sound waves over those shrubs. This current could also be 'seen' (so to speak . . .), like a dark shadow passing by when the clouds danced beneath the sun. Such sound waves, from such a current, from such a river (in a manner of speaking), usually climbed up to the tree tops, swaying the foliage first, before reaching the level of the human ear at the street side. You had to pay close attention to it sometimes, but it was like thunder emanating from a distant patch of sky saturated by a powerful electrical storm. This river was named 'La Chaparrala' by the kids in school, and it was famous because it had lots of rocks, and quite a few pools. Some of these pools were very deep, surrounding the large size rocks from which the boys, and some naughty girls from the town, used to dive, especially around 2 P.M. when the sun was really hot, and the rays seemed to 'boil' the water.

"When the river became more than a temptation; more than a pleasure—when it became, honestly, a rare, somehow dangerous, but an irresistible, and an inexpensive luxury! I remember all this because I used to look at the river every day, observing, besides, the opposite side, at the bottom of the mountain, where a very large size farm was located, refreshed by the breeze emanating from the current produced by the waters, and where healthy cows and beautiful horses grazed. A delight to look at! By the way, on this farm there was also a very large hut called 'El Caney' inside of which the owners of the farm, an elderly couple, used to dry tobacco leaves. A few times two other boys and I, the same ones who 'helped' me the first time down the slope, went across the river, literally, after swimming for a while, to visit 'El Caney' in that farm. And you know for what? *To smoke cigars!* That's right. Mischievous . . . weren't we? We rolled them ourselves with stolen tobacco leaves and some glue we took from one of the teachers' desks in school. The boys used to call those little, deformed looking cigars with the taste and smell of burnt grass, and manufactured by ourselves with stolen property, by the name of *humaos!* Maybe from the word 'humidor'? But the headaches I got from smoking them, plus the nauseated feeling afterward, was enough 'cure' for me! Besides, when my father knew what I was doing and in whose company, he spoke to the other boys' parents and all of them, plus mine, got together and punished us by making us clean the town's park during the first two days of a three-day-long weekend. Saturday and Sunday, can you imagine? We had to remove every piece of dirt, including, specifically, cigarette and tobacco butt ends, plus the unwanted shrubs that were dead already or dying out while still hanging from the trees and bushes. No more cigar smoking! No more swimming naked in the river! No more swimming, *period*! Man, what a life! Of course, I still peeked at the bathers from the top floor of the house, in spite of the fact that my mother strictly forbade me. And you know why? Because some of them, boys and beautiful girls as I said before, went swimming *totally naked*. Even at that age, you know, the naked girls looked as divine as the statue of a female angel that I had seen at another town's cemetery adorning a marble mausoleum. Except, of course, that I preferred the gracefulness of the naked girls bathing in those clear, warm waters, to the 'divine properties' of the cold, hard, crystalline limestone of the statue! . . ."

Some traffic noises interrupted Nelson at this time and he, subconsciously, looked back to observe the road behind Cynthia's car. Not seeing anything special, he continued:

"Well, I remember I had fifty cents, in dimes and nickels to be precise, inside of an empty, small container of menthol. Actually, 'Mentholatum' was the commercial name. You know; I mean the preparation adults inhale when their noses are clogged during a bad cold. It's also something to rub on your hands because of its heat and smoothness!"

"I never heard of Mentholatum," said Cynthia, looking at him inquisitively.

"That's what I was told," said Nelson. "But wait; wait, wait!" he demanded. "I just looked behind us, behind the car, didn't I?"

"Yeah," said Cynthia. "So what?"

"But don't you see?" he answered. "That was a subconscious move, the one I just made. It was as if I was really there, at the place and time I am trying to convey. It was just as if I *had* to look!"

"Look for what?" Cynthia asked.

"My goodness, what a mysterious web the mind is!" Nelson commented.

Cynthia looked at him as if he had just fallen from the sky, but did not say anything.

Nelson then continued: "By the way, in that river fishermen sometimes caught large snakes, instead of fish. One day almost the entire population of the town, practically speaking, and some people from neighboring counties as well, came to that site (to 'El Trincho . . .'), to observe from that 'unique balcony,' all the way down in one of the ponds in the river, a very large snake floating in and out of the water. A snake so large it was compared with that huge snake from those regions of the Amazon . . . ah . . . what's its name?"

"The anaconda," answered Cynthia.

"Right," said Nelson. "I just wanted to mention it because I can still remember that it was on a rainy afternoon, and the river had been flooded for a couple of days, and, also—as part of the reason why that town needed that wall there. Not that the river could have ever reached so high, but, if you ever fell? OK? A very dangerous location, actually."

"Fine," answered Cynthia changing position in her seat. And then, inquiringly: "Tell me, tell me. What else happened to you then, on that Sunday morning?"

"Well—I was dressed in a brand new set of clothes my mother had stitched for me," continued Nelson, without paying too much attention to what she had said. "A nice *little men's* suit. Oh, I guess not really a suit—just a shirt and a pair of pants."

"The shirt was white with short sleeves and the pants

were held up with straps, and reaching down as far as the knee, they had a flap portion in front that could cover the chest if held up, or could be folded backward, and be placed inside, in which case I had to wear a belt. These pants were made out of a soft type of material with a combination of green and white stripes on it. Someone had told me that I looked just like a cute little green bird!"

"You must have been a pretty boy!" said Cynthia laconically, not in a 'complimentary' way, mind you, but as if she knew it for a fact!

"It was obviously a very special day for me, though I don't remember the exact occasion it was," finished Nelson.

At this point Cynthia jokingly looked at him and added some words Nelson did not understand. But he knew it was an instinctively maternal comment that left him perplexed and wondering. "Maybe it was my birthday? But I can't really remember that." And after a pause: "By the way, the street in front of the house was actually the end of the road (a wide avenue at that point), I mean . . . where the road ended (the road that brought the heavy traffic from rural areas and from other neighboring towns into mine)—was ended. But I already told you that, didn't I?"

At this time Nelson stopped talking to reflect on the consequences of what he remembered had happened then, and what he was about to tell Cynthia.

"Every Sunday, thousands of people converged into this regional business hub, in order to sell their wares and to buy whatever they needed for their homes, their families and their farms. I don't know if you are familiar with these neighboring towns, but this town in particular, although it was not a very large place by itself, it was, however, the center of a very rich section of the state. And Sundays were very busy days.

"I still remember how many people congregated, moments after the accident! They seemed to have come out of nowhere! As I was saying, this town, mainly due to its location, attracted people from many places and caused additional transportation problems although its regular population was large enough to have created traffic congestion comparable to that of a big city—especially on festive days. So many people came! Some actually in the late hours of the day before, in order to organize the opening of the market in the main plaza very early in the morning the next day.

"But to make a long story short," continued Nelson, "as I said before, I was nicely dressed up, standing on the sidewalk of my building, holding my little Mentholatum box containing my Sunday's allowance of fifty cents, and all of a sudden, I ran across the street to the side of the river. . . . Oh, boy! How about that? I now remember why," exclaimed Nelson, striking his forehead with an open hand, pausing as to give certainty to his own thoughts, while reminiscing.

"It was because the fence on that side was fully covered with a very special plant we called campanitas in that part of the world, which is Spanish for 'little bells.' It is a twining plant that goes up and down and around fences, covering open spaces, and it produces very beautiful flowers that look like bells. And you know what? These 'bells' begin life as white, develop into violet, and end up in a gorgeous blue—a tender, soft, smooth indigo blue. Just like the special color of the skies on a dry evening during the fall, right before dusk. And, at a certain time, before the campanitas are fully grown, these simple, delicate and beautiful flowers turn purplish, like the waters of the oceans about to mix with the colors reflected by certain corals when lit by the rays of a dormant sun, off the shores in some Pacific islands. That phenomenon can be observed from space. . . . Or in any tropical region on this gorgeous paradise we have the privilege of calling Mother Earth, and 'by golly!', not only the privilege but the honor of inhabiting it now!!!"

Nelson St★ took a long breath at this time, while he continued to observe Cynthia's face for any reaction.

"Were you ever in space, Mr. St★?" Cynthia snapped back sarcastically.

Without making a direct response, Nelson paused and offered, "I loved those blue bell flowers so much, I wanted to give my mother a couple for her birthday," after some silence had accentuated the meaning of Cynthia's question.

At this time and point, Nelson stopped suddenly again, and then said affirmatively: "That's right. It was her birthday! Just by talking about it I can bring back details that have been lost for so many years. It's incredible how our memory lapses, and then all of a sudden, awakens, stitching together those forgotten threads we didn't even think still existed."

"Yes," picked up Cynthia, "I know that our minds close sometimes, keeping inside of minute spaces located in certain gaps, large chunks of our lives, for certain periods. Just like in a computer."

"Computer?" Nelson asked.

"Yes—you want to put aside, temporarily, some portion of your written work? So you 'cut' and 'paste,' keeping the part you want to move to some other location or time, in the hidden space called the 'clipboard.' I am sure that our memory bank is capable of retaining almost every instant of our existence, bringing to light some sections under special circumstances and conditions—sections which our conscious brain was doing a great job at placing in recondite labyrinths for long periods of time. Retrieving those memories, however, is part of growing and developing—but of course, you know that. You are a computer expert and you are aware that computers are but a simple reproduction of our mental abilities, built as a similar, yet not exact, pattern of function from our brain's structure!"

"My goodness," said Nelson, very pleased, "you really are a very bright, and also a very beautiful young woman."

"Thank you, sir. You are not so bad yourself," answered Cynthia.

"Oh!!!" was Nelson's way of expressing his acceptance of the compliment, and his comprehension of her feelings for him.

At this time, Cynthia was driving slower than she had been, and when he asked her the reason for it, Cynthia replied that she wanted to extend the time they were together.

"I like that," said Nelson. "But we can always get together later on, anyway."

"Oh—but I insist that you tell me now the circumstances of that other incident you mentioned before; you know, the one wherein a member of your immediate family was also involved?"

"Oh, yes" said Nelson. "That was with my last foster father. . . ." And then he added: "By now I figure you must already know that I was placed in the care of several foster families for relatively short periods of time, and that the changes from family to family were made (I know now), by the government agency in charge of so-called adoptions."

Nelson stopped to think, almost apprehensively. "Maybe . . . ah . . . well, maybe we should talk about that some other time?"

"It's up to you," Cynthia said without inflection.

Silence then became the only cushioning wall keeping them together, while they continued their ride home.

But after a few minutes, Nelson added: "Oh, what the heck! If you want to know, I'll tell you right now, but please let that be the end of it?"

She silently agreed to his condition, and he then said,

"But let me first finish telling you what happened that Sunday morning. I almost forgot, I must be getting old. Yes! *Senility is approaching, riding on the chariot of old age.* How about that? I just invented that expression! Now don't you forget to quote me sometime!" added Nelson euphorically.

"Now, let's see. . . . While I was crossing over to the side of the fence where the flowers were, I dropped my Mentholatum container with the fifty cents in it. And, afraid that I was going to lose it, I doubled back without looking at the road. And then a truck, with a lot of people in it, struck me on my left hip, and sent me rolling about ten feet away. I was fortunate that it sent me rolling *away* from it, because that saved my life. I remember seeing the face of the truck driver when he pulled the emergency brake and the truck stopped only a few inches away from my head. I don't really know if I saw the driver while I was still standing, and before he hit me . . . or. . . . Anyway! I was lying on my back with my face looking up, and I saw my parents desperately looking down at me from the balcony on the top floor of the house. Then, as if my father had had wings, he suddenly appeared in front of me like a guardian angel, and carried me upstairs. I do not remember anything else about that incident, except that I kept my box of Mentholatum with the fifty cents inside, tightly closed in my left fist, for a very long time."

"Oh, God," cried Cynthia, with a painful, sympathetic feeling in her voice. "What a horrible thing to happen to a child!"

With that statement, Cynthia sealed the moment. Obviously there was not another thing to be said or to be added, and after a few minutes, tacitly asserting the gravity of that day's events when Cynthia hit Nelson's bike, both new acquaintances decided to stop for a while on the side of the road, to calm their nerves before continuing their trip home.

Distracted by the view of the open countryside, and by Cynthia's deliberate silence which was to allow him relaxation time, Nelson closed his eyes and for a moment visualized himself walking along with Cynthia, holding hands together, in the green field of the Olympic Stadium. Oddly enough—that green field was totally surrounded by campanitas hanging from heaven and changing colors constantly—as the display of multicolor electrical bulbs during a festive season, accentuating in Nelson's mind the realization that he had been considering her as someone he had already seen and known before. *Was it that she had also been there, at the moment of the accident, and that she had also protected him from injury?* Perhaps Nelson just could not remember seeing her face there? Or, perhaps, the face of the driver was another way for her to conceal her presence during those circumstances. . . .

Who knows? Her laconic ways were intriguing to Nelson, to say the least. When in doubt, disregard your assumption, unless there's a way to prove it true!

"Morning Glory!" shouted Nelson, all of a sudden. "That's right! Common morning glory! That is the other name of those gorgeous flowers I described to you before, the ones I called campanitas. They belong to one of four hundred varieties of the same species and their colors change depending upon the region and the climate. Have you ever seen them? I really love them! They are so unaffected, so delicate and so beautiful! Just like a real woman should be. Just like you, Cynthia!" said Nelson, with a meaningful look in his eyes while staring deeply into hers.

"Oh, thank you, Nelson St★" said Cynthia coquettishly. "I drink to you" she added, raising her hand in a toasting gesture.

"No, no! Let me add," interrupted Nelson with a hand movement requesting her to listen. "In the same manner in which a woman is the feminine essence of the human race, and the most beautiful side of all human beings, these campanitas are the natural image of the intrinsic beauty of the floral kingdom. And, having said that, I—drink—to you—Miss Campanitas!" ended Nelson. In the spirit of playful pleasure, both "toasted" with an imaginary flute filled with champagne, while giving each other a look of understanding!

Nelson now continued. . . .

". . . During my last vacation I did some work for an out-of-state corporation, and they supplied me with a company car, so I could visit their clients. The corporation got a special permit for me to drive that car, a mini van type, which looked like a small bus. I was sent to see a client who was located in a small town nearby, about one hour away from the main office of the company.

"Since my then foster father was a semi-retired person, I used to take him out frequently, especially on Sundays, when I would go swimming in the local pool or play soccer, basketball, tennis—or just work out in the municipal facilities. He loved to come along just to be outside while I did my exercises! Then we would go to eat fruit and ice cream, spending almost the entire day together.

"Well, on this particular day, I insisted that he come along with me just for the ride. He didn't want to go out, but I begged him. (Strange, now that I think of it!) But he finally agreed and we left. After riding for a few minutes on the highway, we reached a section under construction, with a long and very difficult detour. Everything was fine, except for a car that pulled behind mine a little too close, and then tried to pass me on the wrong side. And when he could not, he moved to the other side, very fast, bumping my car a little. I tried to get away from the scene, so I accelerated. I have no idea how or why it did happen, but the accelerator got stuck, and I could not stop the car! Perhaps the uneven terrain, full of very large holes, broke the pin that connects it? My car kept on going, increasing in speed faster and faster. And, while I tried to avoid other traffic, or to be smashed against a small hill's slope that was facing me like a Chinese wall on the right hand side, I swerved to the left as soon as I saw there were no other vehicles coming in front of me . . . but, at that speed I hit the railroad tracks, which I hadn't even noticed before, on the left side, with my front tire, and the car went right up in the air instead like a runner on a high jump! While in the air, it rotated counterclockwise three hundred and sixty degrees and, fortunately for us, we landed on top of some trees, and on some very thick, strong and tall bushes, that softened the impact of the fall. We were lucky those bushes were there! They allowed the vehicle to straighten itself up, to land gently on its four tires on a soft and green patch of tall pasture about fifteen feet down from the edge of the road, and the railroad tracks."

"Oh, my Lord!" exclaimed Cynthia, excited and thrilled—and also at the same time concerned about Nelson. "That is incredible!" She then touched Nelson's arm, and looked at him with a "poor babe" kind of expression, as if to console him.

"Then we got out," continued Nelson, "and the driver of a large truck working in that section of the highway came down and cut a few barbed wires, removed some of the fence's posts, and drove the mini van out of that place through a private road and onto the main one. The car was OK, except for a couple of scratches."

"I don't believe it," said Cynthia again. "What did your father say?"

Nelson, reflecting on the incident, answered: "That's precisely why I dislike to talk about this accident! My father saw both of us 'dead' while the car was rotating in the air, and frightened, he yelled in the middle of the horrible thing: 'My son, we have killed ourselves!!!' "

"I mentally recorded those words deeply in my mind; I felt them reverberating in my heart, penetrating farther inside of me, causing my entire body to shiver from head to toe, and profoundly digging a path in my soul, where they stuck.

"At the same time, I grabbed my dad during his rotation, and pulled him down next to my right thigh. As I remember, I kept him next to me with a strong embrace, until the car came to a full stop. Nothing whatsoever happened to me. And my father, thank goodness, was also OK. The only injury my father suffered was a small scratch on the inside of his right leg, right below the knee, produced by the shift bar of the double transmission that had lost the round handle ball head that covered it. Have you ever driven a double transmission vehicle?"

Cynthia smiled to indicate that she now understood perfectly well the reason why Nelson had been so reluctant to talk about this accident. But, did Nelson really see it that way?

Then he added: "May I ask you a question?"

"Sure. What is it?"

"Where were you when all these things were happening to me?"

Cynthia, caught by surprise, and looking at Nelson with a long and kind of wondering smile, simply shrugged her shoulders, but did not utter a single sound.

After another small pause, Nelson continued: "You know, it was a terrible experience but it convinced me of three things. One, that I was definitely an inexperienced driver. Two, that seat belts in cars are a must. No question about it! And three, that there must be some inexplicable reason why my life has been spared so many times! And more importantly, now, because of that, I have always believed that I was destined to do something great. . . . Well, never mind, it's all in the past!" asserted Nelson as if wishing to forget. "I know that I will be doing something important someday, later on in my existence. . . . And here I am! On the eve of the end of my human life, I almost got killed, today, in yet another car accident, before I have had the opportunity to perform anything of transcendental importance or of interest to anybody in the universe."

"Oh, no," Cynthia challenged him dogmatically. "Your time hasn't come up yet!"

Then, with a question mark in the tone of her voice, she added: "Excuse me, Nelson—why do you say 'in my human life,' as if implying that you know you are not a human, and consequently must be from another planet?"

"What?" said Nelson. "What are you talking about? The body I have, and what I see, and how I feel, are irrevocable proof that I am human," Nelson's voice carried the strongest conviction. "But, to be honest with you, Cynthia, I do sometimes feel as if I belong somewhere else in the universe. Does that make sense to you?"

"Yes!" answered Cynthia. "And sooner or later you are going to realize it!"

Nelson, absent-mindedly at this moment, looked out of the window, and into the fields first, then brought his gaze up into the open skies, as if soliciting an answer from someone (or something) in space. . . . Amazed at the beauty of the skies above, and wondering how it would feel to fly like a bird, deep into space, the trip home resumed with frequent lulls in the conversation.

"Oh, here we are," said Nelson when Cynthia stopped the car at the entrance of his apartment building. "By the way," he questioned, "how did you know where I live? I never told you!"

91

"Oh, don't be silly," retorted Cynthia. "Don't you remember that I know everything there is to know about you, my dear Mr. St★?"

Both got out, and Nelson said "Thank you, ma'am."

Cynthia responded: "I will pick you up at about 9 P.M. If that is OK with you, sir?"

"Yes, ma'am!" answered Nelson. And bowing down before Cynthia who was laughing about his pantomime, he entered the building carrying his broken bike on his shoulders, after bidding her au revoir.

Never reticent when probing for facts, Cynthia had bombarded Nelson with inquiries. Thanks to her journalistic acumen, he had practically no escape from her line of questioning. But to his favor though, his honesty had produced in her the tender reaction of the female in love. After such an electrifying day for Cynthia, she then drove away, already looking forward to meeting him, as discussed, later on that same evening for dinner.

7

At a small French chalet-style restaurant, as typical as a Swiss cowherd's hut, complete with straw roof, but modernized as a wooden cottage, with overhanging eaves, located on a hill in the upper section of the town's park, a cozy corner table had been reserved by Nelson St★ for his first truly romantic encounter since the deaths in his family. Many other women had been attracted by his handsome looks, manly attributes, powerful personality and extraordinary mental capacity, and had been afforded their chance at fulfilling a desire to enjoy the company of such a male paragon, and their wish for an heir to such an abundance of human wealth by offering him the pleasure of their company, as the flowers from his garden could attest. But as far as Nelson was concerned, most of these women could never be more than casual acquaintances, ships that passed in the middle of the night!

Nelson's choice of the chalet restaurant was a perfect picture setting surrounded by a beautiful garden and adjacent to a water fountain that attracted colorful birds chirping their lives away at sunrise, and bathing their gorgeous plumage during the hot hours of the day. Potential lovers were intrigued by the moon's rays reflected on the serene and clean waters during the peaceful, warm, long nights. The chalet had a most attractive view of the town's plaza, located a short distance away. The interference of traffic, wrapped in dust and foul smells, was dissipated as it rose, by the luxuriance of the branches and of the leaves of the trees in and around the park. Candlelight atmosphere inside, soft classic music to dream to, but with the occasional strident sounds of violins being played outside in the luscious garden, riding in the wind, aimed at piercing the labyrinths of heaven. Wines of crimson red, silky white and seductive pink spilled their bouquet all around. The fragrance of longstemmed fresh flowers perfectly arranged in tall crystalline vases permeated the atmosphere, and the anticipated savor emanating from delicious viands with the taste of country cooking on a wet afternoon. A delightful experience was always made even more memorable at this restaurant. Nelson recalled that he had had an erotic extramarital love affair with a woman who lived in the same apartment complex, about three years prior to his voyage out to outer space. That the passionate affair had caused a breech in his family life had never been totally accepted by Nelson, but his desire for the companionship of an attractive woman was a healthy symptom of life's restoration. Today, years later, this intimate French restaurant served well as the idyllic frame for his newly developed picture of love and desire!

Cynthia and Nelson met at about nine that evening. While sipping their aperitifs with delight, both expressed words of praise for each other's physical appearance, and exchanged glances of satisfaction at being together again. Cynthia looked stunningly beautiful. The jeans and sweater she had worn at the time of their earlier meeting had been replaced by a tightly fitting cocktail dress that emphasized her body's deliciously dangerous curves. Sensuously built, her femininity spilled over voluptuously with every move she made. Even her silhouette stamped the seal of beauty evocative of the loveliness that an attractive virgin girl imprints on the heart of the beholder. Nelson had no escape—she showed no mercy!

Sitting at an elegant table, Nelson approved the sample bottles of the previously selected aperitif, each of the three-part main course wines, and the one for dessert (which were then set aside after being accepted by Cynthia), and delighted themselves looking at the magnificent china that displayed delicate decorative patterns. They also enjoyed the stemware from a renowned name with its traditional beauty of elaborate crystal and artistic designs on the silverware, before been toasted minutes after their arrival by the *chef de cuisine* and proprietor of the restaurant, Monsieur Guillaume Montagne. With his traditional graciousness, Monsieur Montagne accepted the honor of their presence with a "brindis" with the most tasty medium dry champagne served in an exquisite goblet of his own design. A little fruit, accompanied by an aromatic appetizer, first set the mood for the three main dishes of the most succulent and delicious food cooked by the best chef in that region. A touch of this, a taste of that, and the flavor of the other, made up the nutritious entrées, the specialty of the house, which was the traditional "three in one" dinner, a uniquely styled menu. As the name of the dish implies, there were three different kinds of viands in order to appeal to all the palates of the exclusive clientele. Plus, sipping the right wines along with each mouthful was indeed a memorable experience. Nelson and Cynthia agreed that they had both tasted "glory" (so to speak), served under the most attractive conditions and elaborate circumstances. "Glorious food" actually, that had been obviously prepared under the careful direction and scrutinizing eye of an internationally known and respected gourmet, for an angel's pleasure.

Among other topics, the conversation during the entire dinner centered on the two other episodes that had made him feel so sad before. . . .

". . . In one of the towns I visited while on vacation," went on Nelson, "I had a friend with four sisters. They were very attractive and all were older than he was. The youngest one was almost eighteen and, I should add, easily the prettiest girl around. Also, extremely smart! Each one of the sisters was between two and four years older than the next younger one. But this young girl—well, I must say that every once in a while I had dreams about her, and today I still remember her in ecstasy at the pleasure I feel when I think of her."

"My goodness," said Cynthia with a nuance that carried a note of jealousy while giving the impression that she obviously believed that she had been granted exclusivity to private information about Nelson's love life (retroactive to the moment he had been born). "Who was she, this perfect woman, anyway?"

Nelson looked at Cynthia while he smiled, his expression denoting simultaneous surprise and understanding, and then he continued:

"All four of them had boyfriends who went away to school at other locations but who always returned to spend their vacations at home. These girls used to have a lot of parties, mainly on Saturday evenings. Dancing and staging sometimes a good theatrical production, or reciting poems, some written by themselves, was the main entertainment. Almost every week also, especially on Wednesday afternoons (schools were off after 11 A.M.), they organized either a field trip to a neighboring farm with as many friends as they were able to gather, or an afternoon picnic on the grounds where the town folks congregated often to relax, next to a pond in the creek close by, where everybody also went swimming. It was a family affair; the members of the families of all these friends were always included.

"One day these girls organized a horse riding party to visit the home of the parents of a young man who was the oldest sister's boyfriend, and to spend the night at his family's farm. Rich though rustic, they owned many animals, among them several beautiful horses. All together, they formed a group of about twenty-two people; among them were a doctor and his wife; the mayor of the town and his lady friend, the judge (who was a young and gorgeous woman of about the same age as my friend's sister number two); the bank's manager and his girlfriend; and a few other young men and women from well-to-do families, all of them very intelligent and beautiful people. My friend's family was a prestigious one in town. His father owned most of the real estate in and around the main plaza. No money was spared to make the girls happy. Besides their boyfriends, there were many important visitors in and out of their house, always invited to dinner or for coffee late in the afternoon, delighted to share in the excellent conversation of their literary coterie.

"This day, the family of the oldest sister's boyfriend supplied all the horses for the riding party. I still don't know why they had so many horses—but believe me, whatever the reason, they were all very well kept and beautiful animals."

Nelson stopped here to observe through the window the group of musicians playing outside, next to the fountain, and calling Cynthia's attention to the sounds emanating from the garden, he told her that they sounded like a hymn to nature. No wonder! The musicians were playing excerpts from Ludwig van Beethoven's Symphony Number 6 in F Major (opus 68, third movement; the beautiful "Pastoral").

"How appropriate," Nelson said to himself. And then looking at Cynthia with wonder in his eyes, he added: "In my mind there is a picture of meadows and animals, and people enjoying themselves in the open fields. And just by coincidence, these fellows are bringing us, for our pleasure, the natural sounds of the most magnificent type of music ever composed. I surely feel lucky tonight!"

Cynthia smiled and took a sip from her glass of wine,

holding it in her mouth to retain the flavor a little while longer. After a few moments, she, with a gesture of . . . 'so, what happened?', acted out with her hand still holding the glass, pressed Nelson to continue with his story. At this point, the owner of the restaurant stopped at their table to say in his heavy French accent: "I hope you are enjoying the music. I personally requested it to be played now. As you well know, it is a classic composition, and you both look, if I may say so, as if you not only belong in that era, but as if the music itself was composed just for the two of you!" And then he excused himself, after kissing Cynthia's hand in a gallant gesture.

"Oh, yes! Thank you so much. We love it!" said Cynthia.

Nelson shook Monsieur Montagne's hand and coined a quasi-Gallic phrase to express his appreciation: "It's . . . 'fant . . . a . . . bulous!' Mercy." And raising his glass to him, he added: "C'est magnifique!"

Then, whispering as if to avoid being heard, after Monsieur Montagne had left their table, Nelson asked Cynthia, seriously: "Do I look like a peasant to you?"

"Oh, don't be silly. He didn't mean it that way!" Cynthia laughed with pleasure.

"My friend had invited me to ride along with the group, with his family's approval of course, but for some reason which I could not understand at the time, I did not get a horse," explained Nelson. "After everyone had mounted up, one of the riders offered to stay behind and to give me his horse. But the oldest sister's boyfriend told him, and me, that a brand new mount was on its way, and explained to me that the group was going to be only a few minutes ahead, and to just follow the road, adding that they would be waiting for me not too far away.

"A few minutes after they had left, my horse arrived. I

mounted up and took off trying to catch up with the group of riders. I started riding slowly while still on the streets wondering why my friend had not offered to stay behind to ride along with me. I was just a child anyway, and I had been left alone by the group of adults.

"But then my horse started galloping as if he knew what to do and where we were going (perhaps following the scent of the other horses), so I made believe that I was a cowboy delivering the mail in the American West. For a mile or so, everything was perfect, and I was really enjoying myself. But then came a disaster. And I still blame myself for it since I was preoccupied and actually a little afraid to be all alone."

Nelson and Cynthia were served a little more wine at this moment, and they both sipped the aromatic drink while looking at each other; he, with a mixture of delight for her beauty, and she, with a broken-hearted sentiment for Nelson's story. Both then 'flavored' the moment while relishing the taste of the wine . . .

". . . Disaster happened because I did not realize, until I reached the place, that a small bridge lying ahead, which had been built as a platform, and whose floor was made out of one hundred per cent cement and crushed rock, had been positioned there in such a manner that it was cutting off the curve made by the road, instead of following the road's natural contour. There was my horse, galloping down the road, the bridge was straight, the cement floor of the bridge was slippery, and the road at the other end of the bridge was at an almost forty-five degree angle to my right. The horse could not negotiate the turn and he slipped with his front left leg and fell right down. I was supposed to make a very sharp turn not only to avoid going into the driveway of a house located right in front of the bridge, but to continue riding in pursuit of my friends in order to catch up with the rest of the party."

Nelson tried to explain: "Horses have, that is, wear metal shoes—*horseshoes,* you know."

"Yeah, I know that" said Cynthia, fascinated. "Continue, please. . . ."

"My horse lost his balance, and went down, hitting the bridge's cement floor with the front part of his body. He didn't hit his head or break his teeth—I checked him."

"Oh, my God!" said Cynthia. "Poor animal!"

"And guess what happened to me?" asked Nelson.

Cynthia had been paying close attention to Nelson while sipping her wine, but she now reacted to the question as if it had been asked during an examination conducted under supervision.

"What happened? Tell me, please."

"Well," continued Nelson matter-of-factly, "at the speed my horse was going, and with the impact of the fall, I was catapulted over his head and I landed a few feet away on a bed of rocks. Thank goodness I was able to touch down with both arms extended to cushion my fall! If I had landed on my head, I wouldn't be here telling you this story. I did cut one of my hands, but it was not a bad wound."

"Did you ever catch up with the rest of the people in the group?" asked Cynthia. "And the horse? What happened to him?"

"Thank you very much, Ms. Cynthia, for your kind concern about me," retorted Nelson in the manner of a ringmaster. "It's good to know how you really care!"

"I was joking" snapped Cynthia, laughing a bit loud. This type of banter kept both on their toes during the dinner. The verbal back-and-forth manoeuvres were sparring sessions, which both could appreciate and enjoy.

Cynthia then grabbed Nelson's right arm above the wrist to caress it with her beautiful and delicate fingers. She then slid both her hands toward his, observing with admiration the magnificent piece of engineering his excellent watch displayed, adorned with an incredible array of high-tech and expensive jewelry, a gift from the members of his space team. Nelson always wore this watch on his right wrist to remind him that those who had given it to him would be remembered by him as the group symbolizing the "right hand" people in his life!

Cynthia then locked her fingers into Nelson's while playing with them as a child learning to count for the very first time.

"Oh, that's better!" he said, feeling her warmth burning his senses. Then with an inquisitive look into her eyes as if begging her not to let go, "Now I can finish telling you the bad part."

"Oh . . . how bad can it be?" asked Cynthia, instinctively loosening her grip on his hand.

"Well, it becomes worse," continued Nelson, leaning backward. And after a short pause, he said: "But before I forget, I must give credit to the town's folks for their great road signs. Not that there were any signs at the location of my accident, but there was one sign saying that the bridge coming up was not only slippery but that it created a sharp turn to the right, making the road at that specific point a difficult place to manage. What I really want to give credit to the town's authorities for, is for the wrong way in which they had positioned the sign. . . . Would you believe that they had not only positioned the sign at the end of the turn of the road, but on the opposite side of the bridge as well, making it impossible to be seen by anybody going down in the direction in which I traveled and where the turn was supposed to be made!? I don't know whose idea this was, but their lack of common sense almost cost me my life and the life of my horse. I later mentioned it to the mayor of the town, and the traffic department then changed the location from that side . . . to the correct place, so that everyone could see it before entering that bridge and trying to negotiate the curve. He did it reluctantly though, resenting the fact that he had been practically admonished by a child. I know he was embarrassed because I later heard one of the horseback riders saying: 'Out of the mouth of babes! . . .'

"Another thing wrong was the fact that the sign itself had been painted with water paint in red letters over a brown background piece of wood, probably taken directly from a wooden box without sanding it or shellacking it first. The letters were almost totally smeared, giving the impression that the sign was bleeding, and making it extremely difficult to read it from ten feet away, mind you, by anyone coming in any direction. And actually impossible from the upper side, the side I was traveling on as I approached the bridge. The mayor did say to me, almost apologetically, that *everybody* "knew" that location was a very dangerous place and that even pedestrians had to exercise caution! Maybe that was his personal excuse for his professional slack? But I of course cannot say for sure that it was the mayor who had placed the sign at the wrong location, or who had authorized someone to do it, anyway."

Nelson sipped a little more wine and then he said: "Well, do you still want to hear the 'bad' part of the story I was telling you?"

"Does it get worse?" said Cynthia. "Well, I can take it. Proceed, Monsieur!"

". . . I got up, checked the horse for any visible injuries, and not finding any, I mounted again, and kept on going, riding this time slower than before. Half way to the farm I finally caught up with the group. They had all stopped to have refreshments at a farm house fixed as a business place, on the side of the road. A country style establishment, half restaurant and half grocery store, called 'La Fonda.' There, the 'boyfriend,' along with the owner of the store, inspected again my mount. They determined that despite of having a small cut on a leg, my horse was OK, and we all continued our excursion. We arrived at the boyfriend's farm early in the afternoon, and the horses were taken to the barn first and given some food and water, and then turned loose in the open pasture to graze during the night. Having had a good day's outing and a late picnic lunch out in the field, we all gathered in the large kitchen of the huge farm house to talk, and to tell jokes, to sing and to listen to some music until after midnight. Then, we all had some snacks and went to sleep."

Nelson, sipping again from his glass of wine, said: "Before I forget, I want to tell you something about the people in that house. The father, as far as I knew, was a genius. Not an educated person, but with a mind of incredible power. He was a professional engineer. His oldest son, the boyfriend, was also very bright and was studying to obtain a degree as a civil engineer. But what was the most unusual, was the oldest girl in the house, who was a spinster. First, she did not wear shoes. Nothing uncommon, really, but kind of backwoods, wouldn't you say? Second, she had very small, round eye glasses, with thick black frames, not really old fashioned, but they made her look like an owl." At this time Nelson started to laugh uncontrollably. Then, between giggles, he added: "And third and last but not least, for some inexplicable reason, she always read the last chapter of a book before she started reading it from the beginning. Isn't that weird?"

Cynthia said, defensively: "I don't think there is anything wrong with that! Some people find that way of reading more comprehensive," she added. "I do agree that for a romantic novel or for a book with a futuristic outlook, the writer probably wouldn't appreciate the re-arrangement, but—each individual is different."

"I guess so," answered Nelson, still laughing. "But at the time, I thought it was funny!"

Nelson stopped to reflect on Cynthia's theory for a few seconds, and then he continued. "Going back to my story, honestly, I didn't think there was anything wrong with my horse. But early the next day, when a few of us were on our way to the local swimming pond, I saw the father of the boyfriend, and two ranch hands looking at my horse and inspecting him in detail."

"What was the problem?" asked Cynthia.

Nelson sipped again a little wine and then said: "The poor animal had a cut on his left leg just below the knee, but it was so concealed that we all had missed it. Actually, the boyfriend and the guy from the store did see the cut but they figured it was an insignificant one. But when the boyfriend's father was informed of my accident, he went to find out, and he saw the horse limping.

"There was talk that he was going to have to be put to sleep, because the poor creature was lame," said Nelson. "Oh . . . no," cried Cynthia. "Poor thing!"

He then allowed a long pause before continuing: "Now it is I who was joking . . ." added Nelson.

"Oh . . . gee whiz!" snapped Cynthia. "Thank you ever so much, Mr. St★!"

"Sorry," apologized Nelson, taken by surprise with her strong reaction. "But at the end," he resumed, "after the horse was given an antibiotics vaccine and a tetanus shot, plus a bandage to help him walk, he was released. And we found out that after a couple of days he was going to be OK!"

"Thank goodness," said Cynthia. "But, why the shots?"

"Well, at the time, they believed it was the right thing to

do." And anticipating Cynthia's feelings, "Yes, I know. Brutal. But I was so relieved! I thought about the pain the horse, I am sure, felt all day long while I was riding on him, after the accident had happened . . . and I was worried about his fate. Thank goodness it all ended OK!"

"Oh my, oh my! Oh my!" were Cynthia's words to express her feelings. "I am glad you didn't have another tragedy though," she continued. "I guess it still bothers you, especially after your recent bike accident?"

"Yes. It's still in my memory bank," answered Nelson. "And I still feel bad for my horse!"

"Did he have a name?" asked Cynthia.

"Yes—'Támezis' was his name. My goodness! Would you believe I can still remember his name? And it was such a long time ago."

"Támezis?" repeated Cynthia. "What kind of a name is that?"

"It's an Indian name. I think it was the name of a famous 'Cacique.' That means Indian Chief."

"I know a little bit of Spanish," said Cynthia dryly.

At this time both Nelson and Cynthia were interrupted by the table captain who came to offer them a bottle of wine from a new vintage, compliments of the house!

And while the sommelier was removing the cork from the bottle: "Actually, what helped the poor thing the most," went on Nelson, "was what the two ranch hands did."

"Yes? What did they do?" questioned Cynthia, extremely interested.

"Well . . . ah . . ." Nelson started to reply but was interrupted by the wine steward pouring a tasting sample in Nelson's new glass.

Before breathing in its intoxicating scent and savoring its delicate and exquisite bouquet—and while allowing the genie of taste to come out of the bottle, so to speak—("it was a mature wine graduated from the aroma of its youth"), Nelson jokingly added with a deep, gruff voice, meticulously emphasizing it for better impact: "The two ranch hands went into the forest, and cut a good piece of wood."

"What for?" said Cynthia, trying not to miss a single syllable.

At this moment Nelson approved the wine and thanked both the captain and the sommelier.

"Then . . ." continued Nelson, "they molded the piece of wood to give it the shape of a horse's leg, and with the help of the veterinarian, they fitted the horse with a walking cane!"

"What?" questioned Cynthia, a look of incredulity in her eyes. "Are you kidding?"

After staring at each other very seriously for a few long, memorable moments, with a question mark in their look—and after Cynthia finally realized that Nelson's words were, simply, something that must have seemed hilarious when he planned them, both young people burst suddenly into sonorous and prolonged laughter. Feeling relaxed, they sipped again of their delicious new bottle's wine from the recently filled, delicate stemware.

"You said you had another episode to tell me, about an incident involving a few little birds. Isn't that it?"

Now it was Cynthia's turn to pay undivided attention to Nelson's facial expression.

"Salute!" said Nelson, toasting Cynthia while raising his glass to touch hers in a symbolic "transparent kiss" from crystal to crystal.

"A votre santé!" said she, winking at him and smiling radiantly.

Nelson was visibly pleased; scanning Cynthia's face in detail while he studied her smile and her coquettish expression, trying to see through it to find out what action to expect next from this unpredictable, lovely woman. He then sipped from his glass once more while his eyes were still fixed on hers, and holding the drink in his mouth long enough to allow his palate to relish the taste of it; his tongue to flavor it; the bouquet to be inhaled by his lungs; and for the spirits of the wine to inebriate his soul, at the thought of holding Cynthia in his arms and tenderly but passionately, making love to her! Then, placing his glass slowly on the table, he thought he ratified a previous request by saying: "But you must promise me not to cry. . . . It is a very sad though tender story!"

"I promise, I promise!" said Cynthia, full of enthusiasm.

"All right, good. You do remember what I told you earlier in the car about the town with the two rivers that flow around it?"

"Yes. Of course," said Cynthia.

"Well, this story also takes place there. So, locate yourself back there, in the house with the garden in the interior patio. Do you remember?"

"Yes. I remember," said Cynthia, closing her eyes momentarily as if to transport herself to the location being suggested.

"I was living in that house I just described," Nelson picked up, "and one day, late in the afternoon, my mother and I were sitting in the corridor, on the opposite side of the kitchen, both facing the garden, when we noticed that a couple of beautiful, very colorful little birds, were constantly flying down from, and back up to, a towering mango tree located on the other side of the wall that separated our house from the next one. This was a mango tree that belonged to the neighbors but whose branches fell on our side, to our benefit because many mangoes fell onto the garden when they were ripe. By the way," added Nelson as a joke, testing

Cynthia's sense of humor, "everybody said it was a 'female' mango tree because the female fruit was not too sweet!"

"I don't think that's true. If it isn't sweet, it must not be female!" said Cynthia, very strongly rebuking Nelson's statement.

"I honestly agree with you," said Nelson now in a very serious manner. "Honestly!" he ratified.

Then, assertively, "Anyway, these birds were flying into our patio, into the garden, and more specifically directly onto an orchid plant with flowers of exquisite color and abundant foliage, which was hanging at half staff, so to speak, from one of the pillars that sustained the roof, a column located at the end of the corridor and the one nearest to the kitchen door, which was close to the exit to the backyard. This orchid plant was larger than most, and with plenty of fresh, green moss, perfectly suited for a nice and cozy little nest. It faced the garden, and away from heavy traffic. It was a perfect location, allowing us humans to pass by it on our way into the kitchen, or dining room, and back, without disturbing the little birds. I remember my mother telling me, and whoever came into the house, not to make any sudden moves, but to keep as quiet as possible when getting close to the birds. Not even a whistle, or a soft, abrupt jump in your heartbeat, as a precautionary step to avoid scaring the 'little things' away."

"Oh, c'mon," said Cynthia as if requesting of him to stop overstating things.

"Of course I am exaggerating," explained Nelson in a joking mood. Then, "Yes, I guess I am," he concurred. "But really, sometimes the birds flew down from the mango tree and landed first on the palm tree's trunk in the middle of the garden, as if using it for a 'look out' from where to inspect the territory around it, before entering their newly selected home. Their actions evoked the memory of a passage I had read somewhere about soldiers returning home from battle, coming down the mountains, walking through the fields, stopped first at the edge of the wooded area, climbed the tallest trees and kept a 'look out' of their homes for some time just as a simple precaution before taking the risk of going back into them. Never enter an abandoned castle without previously staking it out! seem to be the words that describe the situation."

Then Nelson continued: "Well, after a few days, the little 'darlings' nested in the orchid plant container. It was such an exhilarating moment of pleasure to watch the male bring an insect, usually a colorful little butterfly crushed in his beak, or the tiny red fruit from the wild Indian dwarf pepper tree that grew in the backyard, to his lady, when he came to relieve her from duty. My mother used to say it was not just a snack, or a simple appetizer; no. No! It was a true demonstration of tenderness; a token of love and appreciation; a moment of intimate contact in front of the babies before she flew out to dinner by herself! They lived as a loving couple, like husband and wife, flying in and out of their home like humans going out to work, switching places at the nest to perform the same loving job, to take care of home! One day, I can remember," said Nelson pensively, and pointing his finger at Cynthia, ". . . one day, the female, that tiny, delicate looking, sensitive, soft olive-green-yellowish color beauty of a mommy bird, on her way back home," reflected Nelson again while looking far into nothingness, leaving the thought floating in the air, and then pausing.

"Yeah, I do remember," he mumbled as if reminiscing . . . continuing on the same thought. "It was on a rainy, foggy morning. . . . I can see that mommy bird now," he went on. "She was carrying a tiny fluff feather, in the same manner as her husband did often, bringing home food or other things. Perhaps she was thinking to feather their nest?

since I don't believe their home needed any improvements, neither inside nor out, especially with the gorgeous orchid flowers and the abundant green leaves of the plant for their house front garden!

"And remember, they had, besides, the entire patio filled with lush vegetation for their full view, though with a limited horizon. What was really beautiful—actually a delight—was to observe the male, day after day, taking turns with the female, warming up the eggs. Until, finally, of course, after, I don't remember exactly how many days, my mother said twenty-two, you know, the normal period for birds to sit on, the eggs hatched, and guess what? There were two more tiny baby birds to think about! But what was the most sensational thing about the parent birds was that they posted themselves as guardians of each other, and as sentinels of their nest, and as protectors of their babies, letting us humans know that they were there at all times. And to prove it, they selected the highest branch of the mango tree as their citadel to keep an eye on the nest, and the palm tree's trunk as a relay station for food—and to rest during the off-duty hours of the day."

"You mean, the birds took over the entire patio and the garden as their residence?" interrupted Cynthia with a smile.

"Yes. And we were very happy to have them living among us," said Nelson cheerfully.

Then he continued: "Following my mother's suggestion, I placed a little tray containing some food and water on top of the palm tree's trunk (actually inside of it, of course, after I had removed some of the substance, you know—the palm trunk's 'marrow' . . .), and changed it every day, religiously."

"What kind of food was it?" asked Cynthia, obviously enthralled.

"Most of the time it was a banana or a ripe plantain and a half orange, or an apricot, a peach, an avocado, or some other fruit, along with some bread crumbs, seeds or rice."

"Well fed tenants, weren't they?" commented Cynthia. "Did you do that every day?"

"Did I do what?" answered Nelson. "I didn't have to, not really. The food lasted several days. Of course, I switched often; one day this; one day that. But the water—yes, I changed the water every day, because they not only used it to drink, but as a bath to freshen up in that sweltering climate," answered Nelson. He made a pause as if he needed to "recharge his batteries" before he dared to say: "By the way, I also left a bar of perfumed soap in a specially made, beautifully elaborate soap dish that looked like a flower, along with a deodorant in an unsealed container resembling a green leaf, on top of a large size, exposed root, nearby, for their hygienic needs . . . just in case they had to dress up to go out to a special social function at night . . ." added Nelson jokingly (but keeping a straight face).

Cynthia looked at him for a few long moments with her mouth open, and while smiling incredulously, she finally said: "What a silly goose you are!"

They both laughed . . . and then, while gazing at each other for an even longer time, both sipped a little more wine, toasting to their future.

"I can't describe how beautiful it was to watch," continued Nelson, "and to listen to the gorgeous red and black male, with a distinctive yellow bill on its bunting type of head, and an elegant fan of feathers at the tail and on the wings, serenading constantly the timid, soft, olive-greenish-yellowish plumaged female; and later on, the little ones of course, with quavers that sounded like the voices of cherubim singing from heaven. It was also admirable to see how this little male bird, a hepatic type of the tanager family common in that section of the country, defended his food from marauding birds coming to pilfer his supplies. Large size black; medium-built colorful ones, and small common brownish sparrows, singing melodiously after filling the crop section of their digestive systems with their stolen goods, were scared away by his attacks. He used to dive against these birds when they were feeding, proclaiming his territorial right and frightening them away. Would you believe that?"

Here Nelson became quiet for a very long while. Then he said to Cynthia: "Talking about cherubim—you do have a basic knowledge of theology, don't you?"

"Yes, of course," answered Cynthia, very intrigued.

"May I ask you a kind of theological question then?"

"Shoot," said she with undivided attention now.

"Do you know," continued Nelson, "what the Almighty said to all the angels and the saints in Heaven one afternoon when He was tired and upset because of the noise they were making? Ah? Do you?"

Cynthia looked at Nelson questioningly and, not knowing the answer, she said: "No, I don't know. What *did* He say to the saints and all the angels making so much noise?"

Nelson then responded, "He said: 'Stop the noise'! And . . . after a few seconds: 'Everybody sit down!'"

"*That's it*? That's the theological question?" replied Cynthia in disbelief.

"No, no, no! Hold on," said Nelson. "After a while, bothered by some noise still going on, He—the Almighty—repeated in a thunderous voice: 'I told all of you to sit down!!!'"

Cynthia did not say a word at this time, but her shrugged shoulders and facial expression spoke volumes.

"And do you know what the cherubim answered?" Nelson went on.

"No, what *did* the cherubim answer?" asked Cynthia, impatiently.

"They all answered," continued Nelson very seriously: "But on what, my Lord? But *on what*?" (!!!). Looking at Nelson with widely open eyes still expecting an explanation of his own joke, Cynthia said, seriously: "I don't get it!" But then, almost immediately, as if something had just clicked inside her, she burst into laughter and commented: "Oh, yeah! I see now. Only the cherubim, hah? Cherubim do not have derrières to sit on. . . . They only have heads and wings. Well, well. *Well*! Very good Mr. St★, very good indeed!"

A small pause allowed both to laugh not at the joke per se but at the silliness of it.

Then, after looking around, uneasily, Nelson continued with his narration of the birds' story, while moving closer to Cynthia in an effort to be heard properly and also in showing a deep need for companionship, for intimacy, and understanding. . . .

"Until one day!!!" Nelson almost whispered. "Oh, what a painful day it was!!! Late in the afternoon, the male became very agitated, and flew back and forth, from the mango tree to the nest, from the nest to the tree, and sometimes to the palm tree's trunk, and back to the nest, many times. He was desperate. It was obvious that he was also in agony. You could feel his pain."

At this moment, Nelson bent his head down, paying silent tribute to the memory of these delicate creatures who had made such an indelible impression in his tender soul, when he was just a boy.

Cynthia, ecstatic, observed him in total silence.

Nelson then continued: "Feeling his sadness, I stood there, at the edge of the corridor, looking at my friend the red and black bird flying back and forth, and I extended my right arm with an open hand toward him, while I placed my left hand's closed fist over my heart, and asked him, mentally, to come to me and assured him that I would give him the consolation he needed, at such a painful moment of his life!"

Here Nelson sipped some wine to quench his anguish.

Cynthia, fascinated, kept on staring at him, unwilling to miss the thread of his description.

Then, Nelson proceeded: "After a long while, he finally went back up to the top of the mango tree to chirp his way with tremulous sounds that indicated deep pain in his soul. The way he cried, Wolfgang Amadeus Mozart would have been very proud to set as notes on a musical staff! It was definitely a requiem! The love of his life; the beloved wife and tender mother of his progeny; his sweet companion; this delicate looking, gorgeous female who had stolen his tiny heart and had given him happiness and comfort in life, *had not returned home!!!*

"The babies died that night!!!

"I tried to keep them warm by placing an electric bulb over the nest, all night long, hoping that their mom would soon return, but it did not work out. I also covered the nest with a heavy cloth, but that was not effective either. The baby birds, those little bundles of life as delicate as a flower's petals left alone all night without the mother's warmth or the father's protection, could not survive nature's designs. Their tender bodies were not prepared to live in desolation.

"Early the next morning, the male bird, the daddy, came back to inspect his home, looked into his nest, and after observing his offspring covered by the cold mantle of death, he left without making a single sound, flapping his wings with all the strength he could muster, flying out of the garden, away from the backyard, through the fields, and disappearing in the direction of the forest across one of the rivers, far, far, far away from home! Perhaps his instincts had told him—in the way the heart tells a human—that he was now all alone in this world!"

"Oh God!" said Cynthia, expressing painful sentiment in her parched voice and with tears in her eyes.

"I performed a burial ceremony in the garden where they had lived," Nelson kept on, "and left four roses on the ground, marking the resting place of the family of all the pretty little birds that had been flown away from this Earth for no known reason, without a chance to fully enjoy their priceless lives, and without any explanation, to a place deep, deep, deep into the heavens!"

Nelson paused here when his voice cracked, unable to speak for a few moments. And after a sip of wine: "I also cut one of the orchids from the birds' private garden—with my mother's permission—and placed it in a purple vase with lukewarm water, on my night table, to remind me of the gorgeous male bird that flew away alone and in pain. And of the beloved female, and of the tiny baby birds that had unexpectedly become the absent family of my childhood."

Cynthia, with tears running down her cheeks, extended both hands toward Nelson, in a tender, intimate gesture to offer him belated consolation.

Nelson then, lifting Cynthia's hands, held both tightly together, supported by his elbows resting on the table. And bringing them close to his lips, he kissed them tenderly. He then laid his head in her hands momentarily as in a prayer for the loved ones that had passed away. Then he finished: "The orchid lasted, just like my feelings of sorrow, for about one more week in mourning, but my heart still bleeds for the loss of such precious lives!" Silence was all that was heard then between the two of them for quite some time.

Neither Nelson nor Cynthia realized that the hour was late. . . .

Having accepted her request to be his exclusive news reporter, Nelson invited Cynthia, while still at the restaurant, to remain with him as his assistant, in order to help him with his training schedule, at the same time that she managed any news about him, and while she wrote the sports column she had committed herself to do on a weekly basis with her newspaper's chief editor. Before departing, though, and to answer his request, Cynthia kissed Nelson tenderly and, with an invitational tone in her voice, she whispered in his ear: "We'll see how things turn out after tonight!!!"

Back in his apartment, Nelson relived intimate, tender, passionate times of younger, happier days with his beloved wife, and of his treasured (libidinous) unforgettable love moments with Stewardess, before the space mission. *Was he feeling a resurgence of real love* . . . or just plain passion again? Kissing Cynthia sensuously made Nelson forget about himself; loving her passionately transported him to a different life, in a brand new world, where he had not lived for a long, very long time!

The aromatic scent emanating from the female in her, irrigated his senses; the sweetness of her lips, inebriated his heart. Her tender kisses; the soft words she whispered; her caresses; all the beauty that Cynthia offered him, imprisoned Nelson St★ within the walls of her femininity! All night long he savored life as he had not . . . for quite some time! In his memory and in his heart, that night—the eve of the rest of his total happiness-filled days on Earth—lasted for all eternity! Very early the next morning Nelson contemplated with pleasure the beautiful, warm, provocative, partially naked body of his new lover, lying in bed, still asleep, before he stepped out for his daily training routine.

With all the time and the necessary means at his disposal now, Nelson started to seriously participate in every possible sports competition. Winning was not his main intention at this stage. For him, the mere fact that he was training under regulated conditions was worth the effort—and the expenses. Cynthia took care of his promotional opportunities and kept the public well informed.

One by one, almost as if by chance, the helpers and trainers promised by those beings during that night on top of the mountain, came into contact with Nelson St★. Some of them simply appeared just before a competition was to start, and registered themselves as his sponsors. Others came to his house in his absence, and drew up a program of training for him to follow during the next preparatory days prior to a new sports event.

Emotionally, the "intruders," as Cynthia called them in the beginning, created a problem for her. She rejected them at first, as jealous as a brand new bride forced to be gracious to unwelcomed visitors. However, after some time, she simply allowed them. Actually, she had no choice but to accept them the way they were, when she realized that Nelson's Olympic options depended on their expertise. Besides, her own career demands made it difficult for her to spend more time with Nelson. More and more her editorial duties demanded extra hours at the newspaper office; and more and more often, she missed Nelson's moments of need and/or of triumph. So, at the end, Cynthia reluctantly relinquished her position as trainer to the new beings Nelson had previously "hired!"

As a sidebar to this narration: departing from premises that no human has ever seen or has shared life, with an "Extra

Terrestrial" (as far as public knowledge goes), the things said about "aliens" must be understood as merely hypothesis, leaving to the actual observer, the decision of how much to believe, and of what to accept, from whatever has been witnessed, written, and/or made known, in any publicized form. Of course, it is accepted as general policy, so to speak, that if one believes that an alien has come to coexist among humans, one must also believe that "it" should *behave* as a human, not only to avoid being recognized, but in order to be able to carry out "its" mission in the best possible way, by performing like humans do. There are, naturally, circumstances and/or conditions that can change entirely such behavior in favor of a more convenient way to obtain whatever it is that drew an intelligent alien being to live with the peoples of this planet. It is perhaps reassuring to know that no one has ever had a real "encounter" (or so the government officials claim), of which he or she has any consciously believable memory. Though many humans insist that they remember episodes during which they were hostages of some "beings" who had come from "somewhere," or who had actually descended from "up there" in a saucer type of spacecraft—in reality, no proof has ever been given. Except, perhaps, what the alleged images of what has been embedded in their minds could show, once those images were reproduced either as a result of hypnosis, or as the idea for a well-conceived piece of art! It makes no sense therefore to try to prove the existence of aliens, and their dwelling among us. No argument could be strong enough to dissuade the skeptics, anyway. But bear in mind that at one time or another most of us have had some experience that could make us believe in the possibility of aliens' existence on Earth, when we could not find the proper explanation for what we had seen and/or felt!

8

The mysterious woman in our story has been there—perhaps, even before Nelson's human history on Earth had begun. We have encountered her at the various locations where Nelson has ever been. Her humanity was apparent during the bike race accident, where she took care of Nelson's wounds. Her spiritual presence, besides, was definitely manifested during his troublesome time in the apartment, following Nelson's moments of deep depression after receiving news of the rejection of his manuscript—and later on at the time he agonized during his attempt to escalate the mountain. And by the account of the reporters who went to inspect the little town where the fire had occurred, we know that the ghost woman had also been (and "had being") there. She demonstrated some of her superior intellectual ability, when she, with concern, zealously kept tabs on Nelson's whereabouts. (*Was she the government administrator in charge of assigning adoptive parents and/or educators and obviously of supervising them, a job she probably had created all by herself!?*) She was also there protecting the child Nelson when he was being shuttled from foster home to foster home, and from school to school, in an attempt to conceal the trail of his existence. Her feminine touch, however, had never been seen or felt, until now. Nelson's memory of her had always been a vague and an imprecise subconscious recollection of images, in the form of a ghost. Although she always appeared with a certain air of familiarity, it is obvious that circumstances had imposed upon her the need to have many different looks in order to suit the specific requirements of the moment.

But the woman in Nelson's story, as he clearly has deduced, seems to have had being everywhere. Ubiquity has been, obviously, one of her most widely used powers, along with her uncanny ability to disguise herself with different personalities, and to revive in Nelson's mind, every time he looked at her, a different type of memory. Every time Nelson "saw" her, in whichever disguise she appeared, a reminiscent thought, mainly of the fire site with the incredible flames flaring in every direction, had come to his mind like a flashback on a large movie screen.

And now what? In the beginning, he did not realize it but, when Nelson finally thought of Cynthia as the female of his dreams, he thought he knew it. He really did! When was that special moment? Was it, perhaps, at the same instant when Cynthia had said good-bye at the door of his apartment building, when she had dropped him and his bike after the accident and had called him "sir" in a coquettish kind of way? For some reason, the attractive news woman had already embedded herself in Nelson's mind, and had penetrated his heart, arousing an emotional torrent deep inside of him the moment he saw her for the very first time after removing the mud from his eyes at the scene of the bicycle accident.

What's more, during the conversation they had in the car, he had transported himself often, as in the repetition of a bad dream, back to the scene of the fire that had taken place almost half a century earlier when he was just three years old. Something was telling him subconsciously now, that this news reporter with whom he was (unintentionally) falling in love, was the mystery woman, the same one who had saved him from the flames! . . . The few moments during which he had the opportunity to look at her (that thirty-seven-year-old teacher), face to face, at the time he had been rescued when he was just a three-year-old boy, had lasted long enough to open up his mind to receive the psychic message that allowed him to be able to keep a permanent subconscious memory of her.

The woman who had saved him from the fire actually was different in appearance from the savvy news reporter, but both, for some inexplicable reason, had something in common.

What was it, exactly? He didn't know. But he was sure that he was now able to identify the woman who had been wandering in the intricate paths of the thick forest of his mind. Had Nelson fallen in love with her in spite of his unsettled feeling about which of her personalities was true? And how had he come to this realization? Was it while he was holding the broken bike, seeing Cynthia drive away with the promise to meet him again later on for dinner that night?

Another sidebar: When was Nelson's decision to participate in the Olympic events finally made? Actually some days before Nelson had received the final notification of his acceptance as a competitor. The expected day had arrived however after a very long time of anticipation, and only after so many obstacles had been overcome. Nelson had used that waiting time to reflect not only on the possibilities of winning, as he had always expected; but he had also thought of the possibilities of *losing.* . . . However, a very strange and very powerful force had kept on poking in his head, telling him that there could be no room for defeat. The more he contemplated the thought of winning the decathlon, the stronger was his desire for competing. He knew, instinctively, that his presence on the Earth had a very special purpose, and that his participation in the Olympics was the reason for something that was beyond his understanding at this point.

The trip to the Olympic site was a quiet event though. Not too many people were actually aware that Nelson St★

had, defiantly, decided to participate—but those who did know were more curious than convinced. Nelson's age and the negative attitude of the media in recent months, had created a vacuum against his professional integrity, and against his possibilities as a championship athlete.

Some reporters did come to greet him on his arrival to pose some impertinent questions. Calmly answering one question: "Who will inherit the medals you are going to win? . . ." Nelson replied that "Indeed, someone will definitely be there to accept my humble offerings of gold to the Olympian gods!"

The press thought his answer had been a joke. And his prophetic words: "The special ceremony of the Closing of the Games will be, this time, something the peoples from Earth will never forget! . . ." were of course, not only completely misunderstood, but totally ignored.

Nelson and his entourage settled then in their assigned quarters. It looked strange to some of the athletes that a person of Nelson's advanced age would share accommodations, but it was even stranger that the trainers and helpers who had come along with Nelson were rarely seen in their own beds. And since everyone minded their own business, it was accepted as the normal thing to do. (By the way, as in all sports events, from the very first day the Olympic atmosphere itself fostered camaraderie; friendship; and even love at first sight among some of the participants; it also uncovered the hidden flaws of certain athletes whose only ambition was their personal glory and lucrative future, and exposed, besides, the many frailties of human behavior.)

Figuratively speaking, time forms the boundary line of the circle of life. But time flies, and on its wings, life itself expands; triumphs are obtained; fortunes are made. And at the center of the known universe, right in the middle of that circle, in a manner of speaking, humans themselves can't stand still. For Nelson St★ the athlete, the moment of truth had finally arrived. The pageantry of the parade; the beauty that was displayed; the festive mood . . . lifted the spirits of thousands of people congregated in the Olympic stadium. As in a festival of flowers, all athletes, like blossoms from the gardens of every country on Earth, displayed their colorful petals and filled the air with their fragrance, on this glorious morning of the day of the Opening Ceremonies.

Nelson St★, the Olympic contender, carried the branch of an olive tree from a historic garden in Greece, as his emblem. And as the anthem of his choice, he had selected a triumphant march composed by him (which he, by the way, had insisted on keeping as a secret 'till the very end of the Closing Ceremonies).

Dressed in white lamé pure silk pants and a long-sleeved tightly fitted shirt with an open collar of the same type of material (a fabric of laminated silver combined with silk that attracted a second look at his powerful, athletically built body); blue suede athletic shoes, a blue sky colored band around his waist, and a turquoise bandanna on his forehead, enhancing his striking green eyes, made Nelson look almost other-worldly during this most memorable Earthly party! He felt radiant, and his effulgence spread light and energy around him. He was as magnificent as a shining star on a cold, clear night. And in spite of the fact that everybody knew his age, the crowd was totally oblivious to the fact. They were mesmerized instead—perhaps captivated by the appeal of his attire, a real champion's suit, which made them chant his name repeatedly the moment he passed by the reviewing stand, as if he had already won a gold medal. His face reflected his happiness at achieving at least the basic triumph of being able to participate. So many important things had stood in his way; so much pain and loss he had had to endure! By just forming part of the competitors' group, Nelson had finally attained his initial goal.

In rows of ten abreast, groups of athletes marched into the stadium following a preconceived plan. Patriotic tunes from the best known composers enhanced the already glorious atmosphere. All over, the spectators enjoyed the carnival of colors, and the variety of peoples congregated. The colorful procession brought joy and excitement to the public. The glamour of youth permeated the stage where the spectacle of strong, handsome male, and svelte, beautiful female athletes, would be delighting the eyes of the crowd. One by one groups representing every nation advanced toward the center of the green zone, after passing the reviewing stand, with the local dignitaries and the representatives of foreign governments looking at them. Emotions ran high, and the anxiety produced by the expectation kept everyone at the peak of their spirits. Moral support was part of the help the athletes needed, and plenty of it was being given by the crowd. Moment by moment every spot in the field was being covered. Pockets of empty space were quickly filled, until there was not a single square foot unoccupied. When the last group was in place, the IOC's president addressed everyone present, and through the waves: "Olympians. Citizens of Earth," he started saying. "More than two and a half thousand years have gone by since, on this land, the founders of democracy consecrated with their victories in competitions among humans from all parts of the globe, what we dedicate today as the stage of triumph over ourselves. We have come together at this time and in this location to celebrate among the peoples from this Earth," and pausing for a long while, he added: "and why not, along with the peoples from the rest of the universe . . ." (at which point clamorous applause interrupted his delivery . . .), "to celebrate the friendly meeting of all nations represented not only by the competing athletes, but by all those persons congregated within the walls of this stadium, as well as by those who pay tribute to them with their moral support, and with their economic help."

After a long pause during which the crowd started to buzz with excitement, he added: "Let's enjoy our athletes' prowess, and relish every moment of their glory, as those Olympian spectators did during the celebration of the very first Games. It is my wish, as well as the wish of every member of the International Olympic Organization, and I am sure it is also the wish of all the peoples congregated to honor these outstanding young men and women competing for their own countries, to welcome all to this new Olympic marathon, and to toast the new gods in this new millennium."

And with the sounds of a trumpet playing reveille, he declared, with a thunderous voice, as if to send the message not only around the globe of Mother Earth but to circumnavigate the entire universe, penetrating the deepest and most recondite labyrinths of the galactic fields, while reveling himself in the boisterous festivities: "**Let the Games begin!!!**"

The parade itself had already exhibited to the entire world the most beautiful exponents of the world's best athletes. Nation by nation, every group of competitors expressed their own pride not only by the display of their country's flag, and by their choice of uniforms, but by letting their personal happiness, and their professional integrity, be apparent. When their national anthems were played as they passed by the reviewing stand, all members from each team clearly showed in their attitude, with their smiles and sharp appearance, the real essence of sportsmanship. Nelson's silent moment, however, provoked astonishment, and made the crowd respectfully observe his personal wishes. Finally, with everyone settled in their seats, then, the Games began!

That first day of competitions was indeed a triumphant one for Nelson St★. His dreams were partially realized!

Nelson however declined to be honored after winning his first gold medal. This action was automatically condemned by the IOC. He had previously requested that any formality honoring him be delayed until the time of the final ceremonies, which the Olympic Committee refused to do. Nelson then had agreed to stand on the winners' platform, with the condition that only the hymns from the countries of the winners of the silver, and of the bronze medals, would be played, and after both parties had agreed to a mutually acceptable compromise. He stipulated, furthermore, that the anthem of the host country should be played, instead of his. However, fans who felt somehow personally identified with Mr. St★, the over-age athlete, were now seeing in this young man of fifty years of age the new hero needed to boost their own sports enthusiasm. So, Nelson's golden moments on the winners' platform without his own anthem to ennoble the occasion, and to truly identify his place of origin, were not as shiny as the public wanted them to be. Problems began to arise.

On the one hand, the lack of luster of these ceremonies created new psychological doubts in the minds of the spectators. Many a fan, not knowing the truth, asked other spectators—and specially those persons in charge of conducting the ceremonies—"Why was the winner denied his glory?" No matter how plausible were the explanations given by the IOC, they did not completely satisfy Nelson's new followers.

On the other hand, sports fever had returned to the hearts of those who had previously accepted him, but who had temporarily forgotten he even existed. Once again, Nelson had become their athlete, and the story of his life was, once more, being scrutinized. Acceptance was not difficult for the hearts of those aware of his personal circumstances. Yet, for those ignorant of his past, understanding was not easy. Moment by moment, however, he regained the good will of the crowd. Fortunately, the Olympian gods had already decided to be more propitious to him from the very first day of the competitions. *Glory to the gods!*

Winning three medals—gold, silver, and bronze, out of the first five events, was an accomplishment rarely seen in the annals of the decathlon. The public was impressed. The other athletes were envious. And everyone was incredulous. The members of the IOC were surprised. "How is it possible," they argued among themselves, "that a fifty-year-old competitor became capable of winning against twenty-year-old athletes, defeating the laws of physics and turning upside down every rule in the book?"

In view of the facts and considering the circumstances, the Olympic authorities that same night ordered still another set of tests for the next day, under pressure exerted by a few nations' representatives. Although tension and apprehension was created by rumors in the press, for Nelson St★ the new situation was simply one more routine check-up.

The following morning, once again, the test results failed to prove any malfeasance on Nelson's part, and ratified instead that his digestive system's functions were normal. The only conclusion was, as it had been before, that his body was able to retain larger amounts of nutrients than most athletes' organisms, and for longer periods. Besides, that Nelson was capable of making special use of those nutrients, as they were required. The so called "time lapse" system technique, as someone had named it earlier. Fortunately, the medical experts, though they had their own doubts, never even attempted to hypothesize publicly about any possibility of an extraterrestrial connection, perhaps to avoid being ridiculed, or even ostracized. Not a single item of evidence was found anyway, to give credit or even to allow such supposition. Nelson St★, the athlete, had finally been qualified and duly accepted!

The new battery of tests performed, served in addition to change the way some of the people were still looking at him. And the new and final results helped Nelson, once again, to go forward to fulfill his ambitions. As a matter of fact, delegates from many nations, including those that had previously denied him their support, upset by allegations based on improper foundation, and by the general public's twists in its opinion of Nelson St★, came to see the Olympic Committee. They wanted also to meet with Mr. St★, and to offer now their support to the gallant hero "who should not be left alone during such extraordinary circumstances!" (It was also at this specific time when the media tried to pay some attention to Nelson's assistants, in an attempt to print a story about them. . . .)

In the Olympic Village cafeteria, that same morning, members of the press used the opportunity to try to interview all the trainers and all the helpers who had come together to discuss the next day's activities. Knowing however that the stories they had to tell could not possibly be believed, every one of the beings refused to comment at all, on any subject, at that time, following instructions from Mr. St★. It was actually a stand-off situation. The reporters snapped pictures and asked questions, which Nelson's trainers and helpers politely refused to answer (and totally ignored the questioners), repeatedly expressing their wish to be left alone. At the end though, after some exacerbating moments, those reporters departed murmuring a few unprintable remarks.

Among Nelson's assistants, of course, was Cynthia herself. Yet, for some unexplainable reason and despite the fact that she had been part of Nelson's athletic team even before the "helpers" and the "trainers" were known to be members, no reporter ever used any resources or personal clout to disclose in any way the deep relationship that obviously had developed between Nelson and Cynthia from the moment they had met. Cynthia herself, being a reporter, knew exactly how to proceed if in fact she did not really want anyone else to interfere with her life or the life of her beloved. Was there actually a concealment of her actions that had been mentally, or telepathically, imposed by someone else? Was there another factor making this Cynthia's choice, a factor that perhaps had something to do with her, personally, or with something about her that not even Nelson, was aware of?

It is odd that no one in the media even bothered having Cynthia's picture taken by any news service. Nor was any specific information concerning Cynthia and her liaison with Nelson released to the public. Was it, perhaps, a courtesy paid to her by her business associates and acquaintances, as a gesture of professional ethics to avoid having her face any particular problems that did not need her involvement as a part of the team?

Whichever the case, the question remains: Why was Cynthia totally ignored when others were constantly pursued as prey? Was it perhaps that she had the power and the capacity to control other peoples' decisions and actions, and that tacitly she did her job so well that not even a rumor was ever heard? No matter how you put it, the point cannot be ignored: she did not exist, practically speaking, for anybody else but for Nelson, and only beginning after a certain time in his life on Earth!

Nelson St★ had spent one day of rest preparing himself

for the next day's events. His mind, however, had kept on unwinding the grueling moments of the first five competitions, and unfolding the strange happenings of that date. He recalled that during the events of the first day, the spectators had taken the opportunity to demonstrate their acceptance of his athletic merits every time his picture had flashed on the big screen. They had also expressed their recognition of Nelson's special skills by responding with thunderous applause at the mention of his name.

Again, during that day of rest, many representatives from several nations' teams had come to see Nelson at his quarters, to congratulate him for his prowess. Special envoys from governments that previously had not only refused Nelson's requests for sponsorship, but that had also ignored him, had come to ask him to please accept now their patronage. Offers to become the spokesperson for special products had poured in by the dozens; tickets for the events he had been scheduled for the first day, which had not yet been sold or redeemed, became hot-sale collectors' items. The entire world had that day, in anticipation, hypothetically speaking, celebrated Nelson's triumph as the new decathlon champion, and every individual in the Olympic Village had unilaterally accepted Nelson's glory, while claiming him as an honorary member of his/her own nation's team. The interest of the entire world in this super athlete was now so high that many other participants seemed eclipsed. Nelson St★ had become the true idol of the world of sports! The first day of competitions had been a triumphant one for Nelson St★. At the same time, his dreams had also been partially realized. Although, the crowd at first had looked with skepticism at a fifty-year-old athlete (labeled "opportunist" by certain members of the press), Nelson's serenity had allowed him to conduct himself with the dignified manner of a true athlete. He knew that the public, in general, is always responsive to valiant deeds, and that at the end his honest intentions would prevail.

As it is common in every event of this nature, a specific section of the crowd cheered the athletes of their predilection. Nelson did not count on any particular group to follow him. No nation had accepted his sponsorship request. There are, of course, those courageous fans who are always willing to back up the weak and/or unknown. Also, there are those honest spectators who would, in any case, give support not only to the weak and to the unknown, but even to the ones considered to be losers, simply because they had the courage to try and to attempt to win. As Nelson understood, "There are no losers in an Olympic competition. You might not be a winner of a determined type of event and/or of a specific kind of medal, but you can never be regarded as a loser. Not after what you have done and gained to be able to reach that plateau in the world of sports!" Unfortunately, there exists another segment, one made up of persons ready to mock anyone who would fail to satisfy their personal, economic and, otherwise, egocentric expectations. From that group of malcontents, loud voices had expressed their opinion of Nelson St★, making it clear that he was not welcome, and that they believed his place should be exclusively among those participating in the "old peoples' events" instead. Their explicit remarks (actually their below-the-belt jokes), had carried to Nelson St★ the unwanted expressions of this section of humanity, and had reminded him of the bigotry that still remains in this world. What's more, the unintentional laughter they produced among the members of the crowd of honest fans whose seating arrangement congregated them near this sinister circle, and who had no choice but to hear their deleterious comments, had increased their sarcasm.

Who on Earth could have possibly prevented this situation from happening, though? Their lack of character, and their vicious intolerance caused Nelson to be reminded that there is always a rotten apple in every bushel. What was even worse was that, from among the athletes participating in the same decathlon competition, several biased jokes were heard. To Nelson St*, those persons were the ones who, by their own statements, demonstrated fear that they would lose against the person they referred to as "that old man." Smiling with understanding instead, Nelson simply ignored them. As he used to say: "In the long run, things always work out for the best!" Such deprecatory remarks actually served to enhance Nelson's determination and conviction, to say the least!

9

The first five events scheduled for Day One of the decathlon, had been: 1) the 100 Meter Dash; 2) the 110 Meter Hurdles; 3) the 400 Meter; 4) the Long Jump; and 5) the High Jump.

Nelson had very little difficulty at all in finishing the *100 Meter Dash* with the group of runners, in spite of the fact that he was lined up against some of the best athletes from countries whose competitors not only had a proven record, but who were totally confident in their ability to obtain that victory. Among the contenders in this event there were quite a few who, due to Nelson's age, did not expect him to be a winner. (Another of Nelson's aphorisms: It is not only important to be prepared physically to be able to win, it is imperative to mentally decide to do so before the competition begins.)

Blasting away from the starting blocks with the speed and swiftness of a cheetah in its natural element, Nelson ran along the tracks like a gust of wind blowing in an open field, leading all those opponents who had never expected to lose, especially to him. Impressed, as well as confused, the crowd stood up and, with a mixture of doubt and surprise, applauded for a very long while. After repeatedly bowing to the public, Nelson then, simply but graciously, walked away. The photo-finish results showed, however, that he had come in second. But when the final figures appeared on the scoreboard, making a comparison between the times of the past years' ten best athletes against Nelson's own time, the spectators understood that they were, on this occasion, in the presence of a real champion. Their ovation was really extraordinary.

Because in his first (and so far) *only* event, Nelson had

broken both the Olympic and the world's records along with the winner of the competition, his fantastic speed and personal style had caught not only the eyes of the public, but also, once again, the scrutiny of the authorities. The announcers could not believe such an unusual feat could be accomplished—especially since it had been performed by a person who had been labeled ". . . an old man of fifty!" Perhaps that suspicion was the reason for the IOC authorities taking their sweet time about retiring to discuss a possible suspension, giving the excuse of checking every record in the book, before recognizing Nelson's triumph, and conceding, in spite of the obvious electronic results displayed to thousands of fans and millions of TV watchers, that his performance had been an honest and honorable accomplishment, rarely seen in any of the previous Olympic games. Because Nelson considered his partial victory just a humble beginning, his second place silver medal was a well-deserved compensation for his first triumph of the day.

The 110 Meter Hurdles was the next scheduled event. Nelson had had to qualify earlier in order to be able to compete against those athletes whom everybody (up to now) had believed were going to be the next winners. His qualification, however, had happened during the first eliminatory contests when, with a special effort on his part, the unusual technique he displayed had allowed him to win the first trial with ease. On the second, a not-required "show of force" but a simple act of presence to follow the rules of the game, his speed had been almost matched by other competitors, but Nelson's point average had already given him the edge. The news media representatives present at those moments were simply astonished! Fortunately for Nelson, these members were a group of selected professionals allowed by the Olympic Committee to cover just for the eliminatory events. They were kindly requested by Nelson himself not to divulge any information about his personal style until the real event was to take place. Although all participants agreed, they did so with the condition that they would be allowed to at least discuss the matter under certain guidelines. Nelson obviously trusted in their personal as well as in their professional integrity. Nevertheless, news or gossip doesn't stay under wraps longer than a candy bar would remain uneaten if grabbed from a "free to take" bag displayed at the entrance door to a children's school!

Television cameras from all over the world were now concentrating their lenses on this special athlete fifty years old. Would he improve on his heroic act in this new competition? Would he repeat his triumphs in the try outs? The press had already deified him in such a way that the public could not wait any longer to find out what was it that made this "young man" of fifty such an extraordinary athlete. The fans were anxious; expectations of his victory ran high. Tension was felt from one end to the other in the stadium. Six of Earth's nations were represented by their best. Nelson St★, the seventh competitor, was also there—but all by himself! Though he was now being accompanied by virtually the whole world (in spirit at least), he was nevertheless, still, all alone! However, you could feel the spectators' hearts pumping with anxiety at the thought of seeing Nelson St★ competing again. A certain anxiety had already pervaded the entire atmosphere. The day was perfect: the temperature could not be improved; a sunny morning of seventy-two degrees Fahrenheit. After stretching their muscles and warming up for a few minutes, the seven tense competitors finally lined up at their starting positions. At that point, total silence interrupted the crowd's enthusiasm. Not a single spectator moved from his or her seat. The referee's gun was raised, the athletes' muscles were flexed. But before the fire-arm's blast gave the expected signal and scared away some of the pigeons from the roof, a false start had sent four of the competitors running wild for a few feet. Tense laughter among the crowd replaced a short, disappointing burst of applause as within seconds, each athlete returned to his starting point. Now, as if a premonition had indicated the magnitude of the spectacle, and giving the impression that they were manipulated by a mentally powered superhuman remote control, everyone in the stadium jumped to their feet. No one—not a single soul—wanted to miss this episode in the history of the Olympics.

Silence reigned all over again. There was no wind. A solitary pigeon noisily flapping his wings, interrupted the silence of the moment. And while flying out and away over the tracks, he led the way to a temporary indication of which direction the race should follow, rising then swiftly over the spectators, and finally flying out of the stadium like the soul of champions from another era, carrying the spirit of the Olympic competition.

Suddenly, the referee's gun blasted loudly. Seven athletes stampeded with the speed and strength of a cyclone. Eight fast, long steps separated the first hurdle on top of the field. Almost in unison, every one of the athletes jumped over it; six more steps, at least, were required by some to reach the second hurdle. But from the third one on, one special athlete did not seem to touch the ground at all except for once or twice in between hurdles, long enough to sprint into the air, and to jump over, as a wild gazelle in the open range. . . . Nelson St★ practically flew over every hurdle with very long leaps, as one would skip over a creek's water, touching down only with one foot at a time the rocks lying there for crossing over. It was just like ballet dancing! Each one of Nelson's jumps covered a length of ground every other athlete needed several extra steps to accomplish.

"You saw that?" "I don't believe it!" "Who is this guy?"

were some of the questions being asked among the spectators at the end of that event. Their delayed reaction applause came as a surprise, after realizing that the competition had so suddenly come to an end. The public had simply been mesmerized! Never in the history of the event had any athlete run the hurdles in the fashion in which Nelson St★ had managed to do it today.

Another Olympic record had been broken. Once more, the world's record had been smashed to pieces. The crowd roared with admiration. Though the applause temporarily subsided to allow people to listen to the results, and to the praise by the announcer who, apologetically, recognized Nelson St★ now as an outstanding individual, it redoubled in strength and length, after the confirmation of his first place triumph had become official.

Bowing several times to the audience, Nelson again retired quietly. The news of his golden victory spread throughout the land faster than fire among dry bushes, confirming him as a sure prospective Olympic champion.

The stadium had now become a melting pot of excitement. Spectators were glued to their seats. Although among the athletes the spirit of camaraderie had previously been tarnished by biased ways of thinking expressed in a manner detrimental to Nelson's dignity as a man and as an athlete, now, few if any, could keep their egos afloat. Subconsciously, the audience started to recognize the fact that it was in the presence of someone special. Congratulations were whole-heartedly extended to the winner. Nelson St★, with graceful manners typical of the true gentleman and of an altruistic athlete, accepted their dignified tribute.

The public's emotion grew exponentially, imposing a demand on the athletes, and the interval between competitions seemed an eternity at this time.

The 400 Meter event followed then. Among those in this

competition were two world champions, and the holder of a previous Olympic record. There was also a winner of the 10,000 Meters competition. An arduous task awaited Nelson, indeed. The press services had already doubled their news coverage, and internationally, it was obvious that people now expected Nelson St★ to be the winner of the decathlon, in spite of the fact that only two events had taken place so far.

At home, television viewers were been treated to short length public relations biographical films depicting the lives of those considered possible winners, and of those who had already been champions in the same type of events. Now, from the point of view of the observers sitting at the stadium, those television viewers really enjoyed the best seats and the most comprehensive of all views. Although television focuses almost exclusively on predetermined events and on the contenders of certain choice, it still has the ability to show more detail, by simply changing the angle of view, due in part to the facilities for superior technological transmission being provided today. Also, in the opinion of the fans who had paid for tickets, the TV watchers, instead of the spectators at the stadium, were still better able to judge for themselves, based on instant knowledge of the facts being supplied, and on the disclosure of the contenders' past life and triumphs, who among the new competitors was the best qualified athlete. But since the seat of the fan at the stadium does not impact the athlete at all (or better said, *should not* . . .), it makes no difference where you view the competition from. How much influence can a fan exert from the viewing stand? Now, strictly judging by the quality and reputation of each individual contender, whether veteran or newcomer to the field of sports, the competitor still must try to win or at least to participate in the event successfully. The athletes' fan clubs that usually develop in these circumstances have their own idols to follow and they obviously apply certain pressure on the athlete to win. Each athlete, consequently, has his/her own interest in pleasing a certain section of the crowd. Though the club fans may change their minds during the competitive process, each contender still has a following at least from his own country of origin. However, in the case of Nelson St★, since he was all alone, it was just a normal event in which he would perform his best simply because that was his duty, and the reason for his presence there. It didn't matter to him who was following his actions. . . . He wasn't going to worry about someone or something he had no way of controlling. In other words, it is not a fan's decision who will be the winner of the competition. And no matter what the fans know or do, or where in the stadium or in the world they are located, it is ultimately the province of the athlete. (Although fans do help athletes emotionally and psychologically.) And in spite of any previous triumphs and/or the reputation of some of the contenders, when the moment of truth arrived, everyone in the "field of battle" was confident of their own potential—yet skeptical about the final outcome. Not too many athletes had counted on Nelson St★'s capacity to compete—least of all, on his demonstration of valor, or on his ability to perform and to win. Experience; reputation; background; ability; previous success, do count, but ultimately don't matter. So, Nelson was ready to perform, and simply let the results show!

All seven competitors started with a cadence that indicated confidence and understanding of their profession. Little by little however, they streamlined down the tracks. Three athletes with strong strides, and a clearly defined determination in their minds translucent in their attitudes, took control of the competition. Nelson St★ soon adapted himself to a fast pace. At first, though, a battle for the first place did not seem to be of intense interest to anyone. Then, the athletes' steps increased in speed and length. All four runners, including Nelson, now seemed to have become one unit, moving in rhythm as a military squad, with Nelson along with them following closely. The recorded time for the first half indicated that one more world record was about to be broken. After this point though, the distance between the first three athletes and Nelson St★ was drastically increased. The public's emotion ran high. The name Nelson! Nelson! repeated by the crowd in an effort to give this competitor an edge, resounded throughout the stadium with spontaneity and fervor. Nelson's face reflected his fans' admiration, but his position as second to the front group, did not change. The public seemed to have noticed that intentionally, he did not try to overpass his competitors. Was he simply unable to win another gold medal . . . or perhaps willing to give up winning one instead, in favor of the athlete currently holding first place whose record had been impeccable up to now?. . .

The competition was about to end. The finish line was seconds away. The three athletes in front were still glued to each other as one unit, only inches away from each other. Then, with a tremendous burst of energy, Nelson sprinted, lining up alongside the two in front. Immediately, the competitor in third position, emulating Nelson's move, jumped in front of the group effectively eliminating the adversaries. In a single move, as puppets wired with the same strings and lifted by a gigantic hand, the crowd jumped up onto their feet, and their feelings were expressed with a roar.

In a flash, the match was over. A photo finish established that competitor number three had been the winner. Nelson came in fourth. The runner who had propelled himself into first place during most of the event, registered as third. The silver medal went to the one who had been in second place from the beginning. The ovation was grand. As far as the public was concerned, Nelson St★ had repeated his heroic act. A fourth place finish, under those conditions, was practically equal to a gold medal. With continuously resonant applause, they gave Nelson a well-deserved congratulation, which extended for the length of the time he was in the open field. But "To Caesar what belongs to Caesar!" The winner was properly honored by the crowd as well.

Nelson's triumph, even though secondary, increased his popularity tremendously. His fame was also increased exponentially. His humble acceptance of his honors, however, remained the same. For some reason that nobody quite understood, glory of itself did not seem to arouse Nelson's emotions. He was aware, of course, that glory is something to be conquered, not something bestowed upon you. But, here again! Was Nelson thinking as a human competitor? No—glory did not impress Nelson. The spectators somehow knew it . . . and they loved him for it even more!

It was now early in the afternoon. The next event was the *Long Jump* competition. Through the mind of Nelson St★, as if seen on film during projection, years of Olympic contests went by, and names of competitors and their daring and valiant deeds, started to unfold. Nelson had a perfectly clean picture of those two athletes whose ten years of duelling had ended with the final triumph of the underdog after many events, on an island in the Pacific, during a not too remote world championship event.

In Nelson's superior, photographic mind, on a time sequence, were displayed the images of the first Olympic competition ever recorded for posterity. Even those images from the very first Olympics were, through a recollection of the history books' narrative, fixed clearly in his memory. Or was it perhaps that in his mind there existed, deeply embedded in one of its labyrinths, the memory of all those times since Hercules founded the Games by challenging his brothers to race in honor of their father Zeus, when he overcame Khronos at Olympia? Call it then, reminiscing! But on this day, at this time, at this moment, Nelson's concentration was required to occupy instead all the space in his mind relating specifically to any records of the upcoming competition: the *Long Jump*!

Since the time Nelson had started skipping over puddles as a kid, in the towns where he lived during his elementary school days, jumping had become one of his main hobbies. As it happened, he had always considered the Long Jump one of his favorite sports. In fact, in recent years as an adult, he had been able to greatly improve his performance by his concentrated training. Nelson always reasoned that the Long Jump was also an excellent way to prepare for the Hurdles event as well, due to the fact that one should be able to jump a certain length of space as well as height, when you run the latter. Nelson had proven that theory correct, earlier that same day! It had always been good training for both sports. Although good and bad times had formed part of Nelson's childhood experiences, he believed that some of those moments (good or bad as they might have been), were not only an unerasable memory of his human life, but something he still remembered with pleasure anyway, as an integral part of his existence on this Earth. . . .

The "worst" one, Nelson recalled, had occurred when he was ten. He had accepted an invitation from two of his new young friends from the town he had just come to live in, to go to a nearby creek on the outskirts of the town where a sort of a canal had been dug during the construction of an aqueduct. The digging had accidentally created a kind of swimming pond. Although forbidden to go swimming in that pool, boys from the town had made it into a recreational spot for after school activities. "Look out" guards were even posted to alert the swimmers when the police officers came around to inspect the location. The time of the day Nelson went there however, was during the early morning hours when the other boys were still in class. The invitation had been made specifically by the older of the two guys, a young man whose reputation as a bully was well known in town. This individual's cheek on the right side of the face was covered with a large size patch of blue-black color skin, like a huge birth mark that made him look as a menace. Everybody in school was either afraid of him or resented him for something he had done. Nelson was already considered the best jumper in school, and his fame had aroused the curiosity, and perhaps the jealousy, of this particular "friend." The other boy simply went wherever the "ruffian" went.

When the three boys arrived at the construction site, they found that the entire area had been fenced in, but that some openings had already been cut into the mesh. Nelson and friends sneaked in, anyway. For a while, all three sat down to chat making fun of the rest of the kids (poor devils), who had to be in school. Oh, by the way, one of the two friends had some candies, and the three of them spent some time sorting them out, and removing them from their wrappings. The younger boy found some large size leaves and spread the candies on them, displayed as if he was offering them for sale. Actually, he intended to have them ready to give to the winner of the competition. "Competition," you said? Yes! That was the reason Nelson had been invited, mind you. After a while, the bully dared Nelson to swim in the pond, which he declined to do. Not that he was afraid of the water, nor that he did not know how to swim, having learned when he lived in that town with the river running all the way down at the bottom of the precipice, across from his house. Nelson didn't accept just because it seemed "out of whack!" Being called a chicken, though, Nelson felt he needed to prove himself some way. At that point, the other boy suggested to compete instead, by jumping the width of the canal. And to make it more interesting, to do it with clothes off. . . . At first, Nelson hesitated, thinking that the boys were just going to take his clothes away and leave him to go walking naked into town. But, as the daring persisted, and he got their promise that they would not do such a thing, he agreed. It was a challenge Nelson could not resist.

Accustomed as he was to jump over puddles, and to go up and down the hills and roads around the towns he had lived in, Nelson thought the event would be a piece of cake. He had not realized that a plot had actually been concocted, in advance, to make him pay the price for his fame and expertise!

The young ruffian jumped first. He had no problem. Nelson's turn came next. In order to give him an edge, a kind of diving board platform was fixed. It consisted of a strip of wood, a board of about fourteen inches wide by six feet long, and two cement blocks, more like two bricks made up of cement and crushed rocks, loosely tied together by the waist belt that belonged to the ruffian, since he was the biggest, to elevate the board. Nelson actually thought that it would allow him a jump of a better length, as the third boy had suggested. In reality it was done to throw his balance off, instead!

After the preparations were finished and Nelson had removed all his clothes, he moved away from the platform and, going back as far as the fence allowed him, he sprinted with all his agility and experience. He reached the board, stepped onto it, and pushed as hard as he could, forward and high. But the platform collapsed at the instant Nelson touched the edge of the board over the water, sending him flat on his belly into the middle of the canal.

More frightened than outraged, Nelson came out of the water crying like a toddler, and promising to make them pay. The two friends however were laughing their heads off. Once out of the pond, dripping like a wet rag in spite of his nakedness, Nelson realized that it all had been just a friendly prank. For their delinquency, the three boys received their worst punishment of that year when the incident became known. Detention for three days after school classes, and a very special type of extra homework in math, history and social studies. Also, at home, later, Nelson was deprived of his weekly allowance which affected him more than the "intellectual" punishment he had suffered in school. Was it a really bad experience, or just another step in Nelson's climb to adulthood, innocently played by boys, which supplied instead a good lesson in disguise!?

Nelson's "good" experience though happened during his last year of high school at a private institute for exceptionally qualified students. This place was actually an elite center—(an intellectual hub with branches all around the region . . .), where some very special youngsters could combine all four years of high school with the first two or three of college. In this environment many students were being prepared for government positions and for certain kinds of jobs with a couple of extremely rich and very private organizations very few people were aware of, and under rules and regulations exclusively imposed on them. The purpose was to obtain the kind of individual needed for certain specific work designed for very special missions, with top secret clearance for everyone else on Earth. And Nelson St★ happened to rank as the number one student during the entire curriculum! It was a very private and specialized type of school, run by a very secret bureau of the federal government; under the excuse that all the students were alleged children of government employees. It was built for exclusive attendance by individuals of proven intellectual category, and only with professors with Ph.D. degrees as teachers. It must be also explained that Nelson, along with a very select group of boys and girls, had an open scholastic curriculum that demanded constant travel from one town to another, under the provisions of the federal government, in order to meet specific needs under specific circumstances. These young people did not attend school in the old fashioned manner. The amount of days and hours spent on learning each subject depended on individual academic needs and the personal ability of the student. Learning was not restricted to one single classroom either. Their private campus size, speaking in mathematical values (pardon the exaggeration . . .), was not as large as their Intelligence Quotient though! However, these campuses (which included not only the house but the front garden and the large size backyard of each instructor's residence), were located in several different towns, depending upon the subject of study and the needs of the student. By the way—all of Nelson's foster parents mentioned previously were actually individuals with Ph.D. degrees who were at the same time Nelson's instructors of specific academic subjects. That partially explains why Nelson was moved to different locations; from home to home; and why he was assigned to different foster families.

On the first Wednesday of the month, every student was sent on an entire day's field trip. Scouting, in this case, dividing the students into several groups, each with a specific mission to accomplish, was part of the "sport" practiced that day. For instance, the sending of a certain number of individuals to an unknown location, individuals who were to follow the first group after a certain minimum waiting time, and who were kept behind earlier and consequently delayed on purpose, served to teach the students how to be independent and to be able to arrive at their own conclusions. Especially—finding out at their arrival that it was not the right destination, taught them besides to be on the alert for false information. Instructing them simply by using signals that were previously marked on the ground for them to follow, or built with rocks and/or branches of trees, following a prearranged symbol code, was a good way to hone their ability to recognize identifiable items and subjects for strategic functions. And when they were sent wherever the location might have been (especially to a wrong place), with the intention of getting information that could be used later on to find the right destination, was the ultimate motive to learn how to think in advance before committing yourself—or others under your direction—to follow instructions. Collecting rocks and constructing walls, and mending fences, or putting into practice their new ideas in building special corrals or barns, or changing tiles on the roof of the house, to help the owner of the farm they went to visit, was recompense for allowing the school to spend a day in those fields, and a way for the students to practice their skills. Picking fruits and/or vegetables so that the farmer could re-plant the orchards on time; running, jumping, climbing trees, diving, swimming, playing soccer and football, collecting wood from the nearby forested areas; cooking lunch in the field, learning how to survive in the open, or in the wooded areas—were all routine outside activities during those school days. The other Wednesdays of the month though, only the afternoons were off. During those half days off, however, and the other very special days like weekends and holidays that everybody looked forward to enjoy, and when the students were given time off to be spent any way they pleased, but could not leave the school to go to the field because of the weather—those days became Nelson's childhood's entertainment days. Watching the heroes from classic jungle adventure movies, besides westerns and musicals, or the re-runs of every television program concerning science and space exploration, expanded the already vast horizon of Nelson's powerful mind. He also enjoyed programs containing any information about nature, some comedies classified as "socially redeeming situations," and playing table games of skill (chess for instance), where every subject in the school's curriculum was represented by the elaborate figurines.

Concentrating on the liberal arts subjects of his predilection, such as drawing, sculpturing, photography, playing musical instruments, even singing as a member of the school glee club, etc., opened, besides, new avenues for Nelson's knowledge-absorbent brain. Other heroes, the more modern ones, product of the electronic boom, impressed Nelson very much, but they were unfortunately restricted by the school to a lesser amount of time each week.

He grew up watching his hero's personal bravery in battles among the creatures of nature . . . Call him soft at heart—but he did prefer to watch those heroes who protected nature and its creatures rather than those who imposed their personal power or community's requirements over otherwise defenseless beings.

He enjoyed watching the fearless ways in which the gunslinger with a badge for permit and the speed of lightning on the trigger as means, disposed of the "bad guys." By the same token he also felt sorry when he looked at accounts depicting humanity invading the open lands of the American West and other regions of the Earth possessed by the Native Peoples who were born there and who used to live in those territories, despoiling them of land and of life. . . .

All of this entertainment Nelson enjoyed in the company of other boys and girls from towns of his own state, from the rest of the country, and from some other parts of the world, who were also attending the same institute.

Above all, Nelson excelled at each and every sport he practiced. The school's authorities recognized his abilities, and he was appointed captain of both the soccer team and the basketball team.

As the winner of a singles tennis championship among the schools in the region, he was also placed at the head of the gymnastics class as assistant to the director for two two-hour classes every week, for two full consecutive school years.

In that last year of his high school studies, to celebrate the visit of one of the school's distinguished alumni who had been elevated to an important post in the church's hierarchy, the administration organized a sort of "Mini Olympics" on the first Wednesday of the first month of spring, . . . instead of holding the usual monthly field day. All kinds of sports competitions were scheduled, in which Nelson participated not only as an athlete, but also as a member of the organizing group.

On three occasions he was a competitor, and three times he took first place in his event (the Long Jump), each time improving his previous score. Although the marker numbers might have been down-scaled in keeping with the youth and inexperience of the students, the fact remains that Nelson's triumphs gained him the honor of shaking the hand of the famous guest, and made him the recipient of a special book as the winner's prize!

Regaling himself with childhood memories was indeed Nelson's best incentive; but then, the clear voice on the loudspeaker brought him back to reality at this crucial time of his athletic career. The moment had arrived for him to demonstrate once again his abilities, this time in the *Long*

Jump. Many competitors whose scores were below the expected marks had been already eliminated. Only three jumpers remained, including himself.

Nelson had great respect for the other two, but he did think he could win. In his heart he knew it, and in his mind there was never any doubt about his own superior abilities. He had always kept in mind the encouraging adage: "If you don't expect to win, you have already lost!"

The sun was shining above. The stadium was packed. The crowd fell silent. As in a previous competition, there was no wind. Cleared by the judges, Nelson stood at the end of the runway ready to start his sprint. Nervous tension was felt by everyone whose eyes were fixed on this event's outcome. Deeply breathing for several seconds as if to refill his powerful lungs, Nelson raised his arms for an instant. Then, dropping them down with incredible force, he launched forward with all his might. A strong leap . . . with every step. A fast gait . . . more like a gallop. Perfect rhythm. In unison . . . soul, mind and body battled inertia and nature's elements in an attempt to cover the gap between the start and the finish lines without being concerned with time as a component of the winning formula.

The electronically controlled sign on the stepping board indicated that Nelson's foot was on the perfect mark; the speed and strength with which Nelson hit the launching pad, were simply incredible. The elevation of his body in flight was such that many spectators confused the long jump with a training demonstration for the high one. Virtually walking on air, his stride should have carried him well beyond the highest number marker on the track, as was expected of him. (During his high school days, Nelson had jumped so high, in an attempt to go so far, that neither the public nor the judges were able to immediately adjust to reality.) Thunderous applause then, interrupted the silence of the moment. A short while before, the other two athletes had taken their best shot. And as Nelson could see, they had performed at their peak, forming with him the trio winner of the competition. And there was no doubt in his mind that he had achieved the highest score among the competitors.

Unfortunately, a technical aspect in his performance had opened a margin for error that brought the decision in favor of the other two athletes. His propellant foot step, the last one on the ground, was deemed to have been off the launching pad. So Nelson did not win the highest honor. The crowd felt his loss as a stabbing wound, and long, deep, resonant sighs expressive of sadness, followed by a strong booing filled the air. Still, he was awarded his third medal of the day. (Although it was only the bronze, its value was enhanced by the winners of the gold and of the silver medals whose demonstration of nobility, in the midst of a sporting delirium at seeing Nelson's achievement and under the most eloquent expression of love and recognition by the crowd, forgot their professional composure and carried him on their shoulders around a section of the stadium. Bronze, for once, did shine then brighter than silver or gold.) An Olympic moment never to be forgotten!

The first day of grueling events was now coming to an end. The fifth and last competition for the day was scheduled to be the *high jump*—a difficult and nerve wracking sport. For some reason, people observing competitors on the high jump, seem to know, at the moment the athlete takes those long strides just before jumping, that the jumper is not going to make it, and they tighten up hoping to transmit positive energy to the competitor (psychologically and telepathically) for the athlete to be able to rise to the occasion, and to succeed in his attempt at the moment of going over the obstacle.

Nelson was apprehensive about this challenge. He was not afraid of being hurt; it was simply another childhood memory that impeded this time instead on his ability to perform. The reason was an early experience that taught him caution, and that hindered him from developing the full potential needed to achieve victory in this sport. . . .

Again, on vacation time, off and away from the private institute he was attending, Nelson got together during a couple of weeks one year with some old friends in that same small town near the place where he had been born—the town in which both the bike accident, and the bird incident, had taken place some time before.

Although the behavior of these boys was in every aspect of the word perfectly acceptable, each and every one of these friends had nevertheless, his own peculiarities—to say the least. For example, among them were two brothers who could catch fish by hand in the ponds of the rivers that ran parallel to each other and around the town (that beautiful town Nelson considered a paradise). They did it simply by "driving" the fish into small spaces underneath the rocks, especially in the deep ponds, making noises by striking two stones against each other under water. Then, slowly approaching, covering every possible exit, sometimes using their own shirts and pants, or a large burlap sack or bag, and forming a cup with their own two hands put together, they dug into the dark crevices in the caves. These two brothers were able to submerge and to hold their breath for over three minutes at a time. Another friend had the ability to run up and down the trunk of a tall palm tree with almost the speed and agility of a monkey. This young man made extra money by placing salt among the shoots at the top of the palm tree so that the trunk could absorb the salt as a nutrient. This was done about once every six months to each mature palm tree in town, in order to give flavor to the fruit, the coconut. Everyone in the town knew that. . . .

The fourth boy, however, was a new friend to Nelson St★, a person who attended school in a larger town where coeducation (as he put it) was allowed. This privilege gave him bragging ammunition which he used to "shoot off his mouth" while boasting about his many girl friends. Neither Nelson nor his other friends ever believed these extravagant stories, but enjoyed nevertheless the pleasure of the narration, which always sounded like episodes from cheap novels, or seen in low budget movies. Despite his obvious exaggerations, Nelson considered it a rare pleasure to have had the opportunity of meeting him.

This young fellow was about Nelson's age and had a certain physical resemblance to Nelson, but Nelson was a little taller and more athletically built. It is appropriate to mention that, though Nelson's competitiveness in sports was well known to all of his friends, he, on the other hand, did not know anything about the new fellow's ability to perform on the high jump.

While getting ready for a three day special holiday weekend, the two brothers' parents invited a group of their sons' friends to come along with them. Nelson, his new friend, and another boy from the same town gathered together some camping gear and, early the next day, the group went off to enjoy a long outing in the country side, while visiting the farm that belonged to the grandparents of the two brothers.

During their half-day walk to the farm, where they were to spend a couple of nights, all the boys in the group enjoyed mimicking some of the competitions of the sports they routinely practiced in school. After each event there was of course one "champion" crowned by the other boys. The day went by filled with joy and adventure. Having arrived early in the afternoon, they all had time to perform some farm chores before they were treated to a festive dinner. In spite of the fact that the boys were strongly advised by the grandparents to go to bed early in order to be able to rise with the farm animals, that first day's evening and night, until the early hours of the next day, were spent instead reminiscing about the fun they had that day all together.

Early the following morning, however (at the crack of dawn), they were awakened to perform the chores required to take care of the farm's animals, and (as the grandfather had said the night before) to "earn their keep!" But after the work was finished, they were free to enjoy themselves in any pastime they pleased. First they went swimming and fishing in the pond of one brook that runs nearby. The two brothers had, during a previous vacation, built a beautiful large-size pool in the middle of the narrow creek that divided their property with someone else's land. They told Nelson that during the summer of the previous year, they had cut a few branches from the larger trees (with the grandfather's consent, of course), and after whittling some pointed sticks with the strongest, built a wall, covered with sheets of zinc, serving as the slices of bread surrounding the meaty part of the sandwich, which were the burlap bags full of sand that were actually the wall itself, in the middle of the creek, and reinforced it with some rocks moved from some other section of the brook.

Although the wall had been built some months before, the parapet still looked very strong, and the pond they had dug was deep enough to dive into, in spite of the fact that the creek had flooded once or twice since, and had partially broken the retaining wall. The brothers, along with their grandfather, were spawning fish in the creek already. Climbing some trees, and collecting fruits from the farm's abundant selection, took a couple of extra hours. All the boys were having fun with their individual activities—telling jokes, and laughing in a silly manner. But then, a simple dare became the tragic subject of the rest of their afternoon's amusement!

It happened when Nelson, inadvertently jumped as a matter of routine practice over a four-strand barbed wire that separated the open field from a vegetable garden. Although applauding along with the others, Nelson's new friend said, sarcastically: "Congratulations! But that's not much of a jump."

"Oh, really?" said Nelson, stung. "I suppose you can do better?"

"Yes; yes. I assure you, I can do much better than that!"

This tactless remark then triggered a very serious controversy to find out which of the two of them, was really the best jumper.

Nelson's proven school athletic record, and his on-the-spot demonstration, seemed to have given him the advantage with the two brothers. But that did not find acceptance with the new friend who, upset in the middle of a heated conversation that prompted the dispute which resulted in the challenge, mentioned casually that he had been given the honorary nickname "Cherub," simply because when he had jumped in a special competition in school, someone had remarked that he had reached so high that he could have had touched the skies! . . . For Nelson, of course, the height of his own jumps (rather than anyone else's) was the true challenge. In any case, the challenge was real. But since it was getting dark, preparations were made to compete on the following day instead. One of the brothers decided to become an assistant timekeeper, while the other one served as the judge. Then they would exchange positions for the second jumper's turn. The fifth boy remained neutral. Sadly, however, it must be noted that the camaraderie of the first two days was, all of a sudden, tinted by a touch of rivalry.

That second evening everyone went to bed early. Tension could be sliced into chunks. A curtain of silence had closed between the two contenders separating even the judge and the assistant from the two protagonists. Meanwhile darkness fell onto the stage of the next day's jumpers who were interrupted by an incessant ringing of the telephone, asking for information about the upcoming event.

Needless to say, no one slept very well that night—except, of course, the boy who remained neutral who, by the way, was answering the phone calls until very late that evening.

Just before dusk the news of the impromptu competition had spread to a few neighboring farms located a short distance away. This boy who wanted to remain neutral had used his nascent public relations "know-how" and had called a few acquaintances in the neighborhood; they in turn had called their friends, and the next morning, a large group of boys and girls of about the same age, and a few curious adults intrigued by the goings-on among their children, formed the spectators. Along with them—their horses, the farm's milk cow and her baby calf ('Pandora'); a couple of pigs, some dogs, the chickens, the ducks that swam freely up and down the creek, the pigeons on the roof, and a foul-mouthed parrot that amused everyone who passed by her saying: "Hey you, stupid!" and a goat—these spectators became witnesses to this unusual event.

The news of the "feud" had reached farther than expected! No breakfast was eaten that morning, no chores were performed. The jumpers appeared in shorts and T-shirts. The judge selected the right spot for the competition. The spectators, instructed by the judge and his assis-

156

tant, formed a semicircle around the athletes, wide enough to allow everyone to maneuver properly. A rope was then tightened between two trees separated by a grassy pad for a safe and a cushioned landing.

Cherub jumped first. He cleared the height with no difficulty. Nelson followed without ever touching the rope. Result? No winner. No loser. The rope was then lifted a little bit higher. Both contenders jumped over it again, barely touching it. Same outcome, same decision. A tie-breaking jump was then scheduled. During the preparations, however, someone suggested that they jump over one of the fences instead, and into a corral located a few feet away.

"Fine," both contenders said. Excited, everyone ran over to the other side of the fence in order to have a better view of the competitors in action. The assistant and the judge did not like the idea because first, the landing pad in the new location was a bed of mud instead of grass; second, because the obstacle to be cleared was now too high; and third, it was neither soft nor collapsible . . . in case either contender should hit it.

Nelson studied the situation. He asked Cherub his opinion. Both decided to try it anyway. Some of the adults got together then, and after a few minutes of conversation they came to speak to the group of young people. But no one wanted to listen to reason at this moment. Although the judge and the assistant were in agreement with the adults, they could not stop the "jumpers." After all this, one of the adults insisted that the responsibility would have to fall on the contenders themselves . . . if any bad thing happened! They agreed. A paper was signed, indicating that "all responsibility for any mishap was theirs alone, since they had refused counseling and advice, and that nobody else was to be blamed for anything."

Preparations then continued with the help of some of

the spectators, as some rocks were moved out of the way. Everyone was excited; betting on who was going to be the winner was now going on openly. A dozen eggs; a pint of ice cream; a little singing bird; and even a very colorful, tall and very strong rooster of great prestige among the hens in several farms around, was offered as collateral. The parents and grandparents of the two brothers were delighted with the increasing amount of visitors who were buying lemonade and other soft drinks.

Finally, the two contenders were ready to jump. Nelson went first. Twenty feet run. . . . Up . . . up . . . and away . . . he cleared the fence and landed in the middle of a mud patch on both feet, safely and proudly. His agility invited warm applause from the crowd, after which Cherub's turn then came up. Everybody cheered for him to emulate Nelson's feat. Nelson even advised him not to jump if he wasn't quite sure he was going to make it. But Cherub, looking at Nelson with certain air of disdain for the advice given, ran instead as fast as he possibly could and, with a powerful lift, went over the fence with enough space beneath his feet to give him the idea that he was definitely the winner. The self-proclaimed "assistant" agreed. Many of the spectators thought so too, but the "judge" and the other friend who had been given authority to cast the final vote that would decide the winner, agreed that it had been an even competition since both had done exactly the same thing!

However, not accepting the decision as final, and disgusted besides because his landing had been a shameful digging into the mud, with dirty clothes, dirty face and dirty hands, Cherub defied Nelson once again while removing his mud coat from head to toes, and spitting out part of the dirt. He was outraged. He even cried—more in pride than in pain. This time though, he determined to select the location, and the obstacle, all by himself. But by now, observing

Cherub's emotional outburst, and his state of anxiety, Nelson refused. He had been able to take in stride the loss neither had really suffered. ... But not so Cherub. ... In Cherub's mind there was no losing! At one moment he had mentioned to Nelson and other friends that there had been an occasion in his athletic life when someone had praised him so highly, saying that "he (Cherub) could have touched the skies. ..." That special moment was still embedded in Cherub's mind, allowing him to think that winning was the only way out. (Cherub did not know, of course, nor did he want to accept that certain rules may be broken when there is a valid reason!) Followed by some of the spectators, he then ran down the field and, while still at a relatively long distance away, selected a very dangerous seven-barbed-wire fence that separated the road from the cattle's grazing land, where the contestants happened to be standing at the moment. He did not stop even for a second to study the situation properly.

Cherub did not pay attention to the section of the terrain at the foot of the barbed wire fence; he did not see the inclination of the ground; he did not notice that it went up the hill instead, for just a few feet. And he definitely did not realize that this change on the surface of the land would create a possible break in his stride, at the crucial instant when he had to elevate his body to go over the barbed wire. Totally preoccupied, he was not thinking at all; he was simply obsessed by the idea of winning at any cost the high jump competition, and before anyone with common sense could have done something to stop him, he started running from that far a position, on the down hill section of the farm's land. Everyone there thought he couldn't possibly make it—except himself, of course. Perhaps he was tired from those earlier jumps and from running up and down, but he did not have sufficient strength left to pull himself up, high enough, at the last moment. . . .

Jamming the fence with all his body's weight, at the highest speed of his sprint, Cherub tangled himself among the upper wires as a flying bird caught in a hunting net. The second and the third wires from the top were holding him down by his right leg; his left leg had slipped in between the first and the second highest wires. Screaming in disbelief, Nelson and friends ran to his rescue. Miraculously, only part of Cherub's left thigh, both legs and his left arm had been cut by the wires, and he had suffered, besides, some other minor bruises. Although he did go over and above the wires, he remained in a hanging position suspended by them on the side of the road, but still facing the farming land.

Bleeding from the cuts, and more scared than hurt, Cherub was released from the grip of the fence's barbed wires by friends and by spectators. A round of applause from everyone surrounding him returned then his confidence. Unfortunately, (or should we say, fortunately?) for his own sake, he could not jump again. At that point Cherub, finally accepting with dignity his own defeat, gave the triumph to Nelson St★. For Nelson and for his friends the last part of the competition served justifiably as a lesson from which to learn caution! And because of that, ever since, Nelson had always felt a psychological restraint when practicing this kind of sport.

As said before, the last event of the first day of competitions was about to begin. It was late in the afternoon and the athletes were tired. The spectators in the Olympic Stadium, as well, were about ready to go home. Signs of weariness were apparent at every aisle. Distractions seemed to keep many fans from concentrating on whatever was taking place in the arena. (Call it civilization, but the era of the Roman Empire when the "games" ran for several days and nights in a row, for weeks and even months at a time, are certainly no longer a luxury; however, being able to afford them today, certainly is!) The excitement had been exhilarating, no question about it. And everyone wanted to see every single competition as it took place. But as you know, there is a limit for everything. Besides, there was still another day.

On a par with the other athletes, and along with some of the spectators, for Nelson also while waiting, the instants seemed minutes; the seconds, hours; and the minutes, an eternity. Finally, the competition started. Among the contestants one athlete had an impeccable record and an agility to perform still unmatched in the field. He was not only the first to compete; he was also by far the best. At the end, as Nelson St★ had expected, this special athlete's effort was indeed the highest jump of this event. This first competitor was a slender, very tall young individual, who took his time to perform. After a long while in deep concentration, his stride—a very fast and a very long stride—advanced him so strongly that his jump seemed longer, but not as high. But with the impulse obtained during the initial run, he was able to clear the obstacle with grace and strength, proving once again his already recognized ability in this event.

The crowd immediately responded with great enthusiasm, making him feel as he did, a real winner! A true high jump specialist!

When the second competitor initiated his run, you could see many spectators from some sections of the bleachers departing for the exits. At this time it was noticeable that there was a definite lack of fervor on the part of the crowd, that somehow translated itself into a lack of luster on the part of the athletes.

The second competitor cleared his barrier as easily as

the first one did, but with a little less height, and consequently, with less applause from the audience. Then the third athlete also had his chance at fame and glory, achieving with his expertise the third place in the event.

Finally it was Nelson St★'s time to show off. His inhibitions played a strong role in his competition, acting as a repellent against his mind's wishes. Although he had prepared well for a successful match, he had come to realize that this type of sport was not really his métier. Nevertheless, he did what any athlete with character and integrity would have done: he did his best! Unfortunately, his best was not good enough, according to the judges. The distance seemed too short to give him the needed push, and his stride lacked the coordination necessary for a high jump. Although he elevated himself enough to clear the bar at the same height as the third jumper, the manner in which the judges viewed the way he jumped indicated to Nelson that what he did was not good enough to exceed or even to equal the achievement of the jumpers before him. So, the second and the third competitors having surpassed Nelson's ability, he was left with barely the score needed to win only the fourth place.

What Nelson did not achieve in the last event of the first day of the decathlon was just semantics, in the language of the world of sports. He did not jump in either the style or the manner in which all the other athletes did; he did not cross over the obstacle bar in the same way the other competitors did. No . . . he broke with tradition for the sake of personal improvement, though his jump was never used as a "pawn" in order to be able to win a competition. Have you ever seen ice skaters, for instance, go up in the air backwards, making a complete flip-flop; a somersault; the acrobatic movement in which the athlete turns head over heels in the air, or on the ground, but still lands on his feet? Well—that's about it.

That's just what Nelson did, but somehow different, on a flat way, *horizontally*, instead. Because his earlier psychological trauma, as mentioned before, was still subconsciously cautioning him, he had devised his own way to beat the odds. Nelson went up in the air from right to left; stretched his body as if floating while under hypnosis; flip-flop, so to speak, horizontally, twisting his body left to right; and landed standing up. New style, new technique, new way of doing exactly the same thing. This is not an excuse (but it was obvious that the old way of classifying and of being rewarded was still the only way accepted by the judges) but to corroborate what has been said before: that his jump's height was, in the view of the judges, the fourth best among the group. The public nevertheless had already made him the champion. The spectators who remained in their seats, the part of the crowd that was still attentive to the spectacle, then gave Nelson St★ an unusual ovation after having recognized the merits of the winners of the gold, silver, and bronze medals, respectively.

So went the first day of the decathlon. New Olympic and new world records were achieved; new tribulations had been endured and new triumphs were enjoyed. A new hero had emerged for the world to cherish, and a mystery for humanity to solve! The crowd's mentality had changed, on and off. Its psychological behavior was now, again, in favor of the one athlete who had been considered "too old" to compete. Nelson had been right all along; the public is always responsive to valiant deeds, and spectators love winners. The emotions of crowds swing left and right, back and forth, mainly at their own convenience. In this case, though, the vacillation was in everyone's best interest. They didn't know it, but . . .

. . . Competitions came slowly for those athletes waiting to take part in the latter half of the Games. Rejuvenated

163

after a full day's rest, their expectations ran high. With so much previous training to back them up, and the results of their performances on the first day giving them the incentive, each man's possibilities of achieving success now seemed unlimited.

10

It was dawn on the second day of the decathlon and the eyes of the entire world were again focused on the Olympic Stadium. When the doors opened, a multitude of fans claimed their assigned locations with such enthusiasm that the authorities actually feared for the public safety; no one wanted to miss any of the upcoming five decathlon events—quite a change in mood from the previous late afternoon. Today, of course, was a different day! All those spectators who had left earlier on the first day, were back, ready and as anxious as they had been during the very first hours of the events. Everyone was eager to watch the contestants all over again, but especially that person who was being referred to as the miracle performer of the century, repeating such daring feats as the ones executed on day one . . . at the expense of the best of the young athletes of the world. *Considering the renewed enthusiasm emanating from the crowd, it seemed possible that all the countries on Earth had been telepathically ordered to convoke their peoples at that specific location once again, in order to pay tribute to one very special contender, on that particular occasion!*

The stadium was filled with groups of fans from all the countries of all the competitors. Their presence appeared to be more in response to the results of the previous day's first five decathlon events, in which Nelson St★ had achieved his first three triumphs, and had obtained his first gold medal. Also, without any doubt, as a consequence of the publicity given to that mysterious "old man" whose incredible athletic ability had gone "beyond all human strength!" (as the newspapers' journalists, the TV broadcasters, and the radio commentators had put it).

It was fascinating to look at the people occupying every section of the stadium brightening the atmosphere with their contrasting attires, made out of so many different colors. The impression given was that every nation had specifically dressed up to accept the honors they expected to be bestowed upon Nelson St★—besides the ones accorded to their own athletes. As you recall, many governments had changed their minds and had offered Nelson St★ now their support, after initially having ignored him or having denied him their patronage. Groups of those enthusiasts from the nations whose athletes were competing on this second day had come to the Stadium dressed in clothes depicting the colors of the flags of their own individual countries, identifying themselves that way with every participant, and specifically indicating their location in the stadium. Had someone expressly organized in such a splendid manner, this extraordinary choreographic assemblage? (Bear in mind that in this terrestrial world things sometimes happen telepathically, without our specific knowledge and volition. . . .)

The Games on the second day were now beginning. They started with the name of every single decathlon competitor being blasted on the loud speaker, the instant he appeared on the stadium lawn. After hearing each competitor's name, each group of people of his own nationality resounded enthusiastically, indicating their presence, besides, by standing up, and by waving their flags. However, when Nelson's name was mentioned, a profound, pervasive sound of silence permeated the stadium, penetrating the spectators' senses!

Nelson, of course, did not have a specific group of followers despite the generous applause offered by the crowd the day before. But then, after a few moments of absolute stillness, the most incredible thing happened. One by one with the motion of the human wave, every group from every nation, and every spectator present in the stadium, rose to their feet and, chanting Nelson's name with spontaneous fervor and devotion, started early their never-ending congratulatory ovation for what he had already accomplished, as well as for what they expected he would . . . on that second day of the decathlon.

Having won three medals during the first five events had given Nelson not only fame and prestige, but glory and promises of fortune. Would he accomplish his goals, and win more . . . and consequently, prevail in the decathlon, as he had set out to do several years before? The public was enthusiastic and obviously very sure of his abilities, a fact that kept all these spectators tied down to their seats. No one wanted to miss today's spectacle! Nelson St★, by the same token, was calm and well prepared. In spite of the fierce tug of war of the first day, he was confident that he would be able to accomplish his life's dream. Although the point margin of safety wasn't large enough yet to guarantee his final victory, the total score was in his favor.

The last five competitions were finally beginning, and spectators' fever, as well as the athletes' restless eagerness, was running very high. Anxiety saturated the air in the entire stadium. You could "see" the air reverberating with that deep feeling that emanates from emotionally stressed hearts throbbing in desperation to satisfy the adrenaline rush caused by the expectation of something unusual that was definitely going to happen.

The events scheduled for the second day of the Decathlon, were: #6) the Pole Vault; #7) the Shot Put; #8) the Javelin; #9) the Discus; and #10) the 1500 Meters.

It was early in the morning of that second day, which was simultaneously the last one of the decathlon competition. Thousands of fans had congregated in the stadium again, to personally confirm the truth about this superb athlete who, defying all odds, had won three medals out of the first five competitive sports, and who was considered by most spectators to be definitely a winner. Many had come to the stadium simply out of curiosity. Some so as not to miss the enjoyment of watching "the new and the most incredible figure of sports in the most sensational performance of the century," as the news media had referred to Nelson, that fifty-year-old athlete with the energy, agility, endurance and speed of a twenty-two-year-old champion. Actually, Nelson was a contender with all the best qualities bestowed upon him by every previous winner of every Olympic competition, and with the blessings from all the Olympian gods. Everyone was aching to find out: "Is it really true, he's that good? . . ."

The weather, as during the first day, was sunny and clear but not as warm. Several events had already started in other sections of the track and field, but the eyes of the world were definitely upon one particular sport, the first in line for the decathlon competition: *the Pole Vault.*

Twice during practice Nelson had broken the poles he had used for training. Was it perhaps that Nelson's demands for a type of pole, still under regulations, but specifically made to suit his needs, were never met? Or was it that Nelson's "climbing" on the pole itself debilitated its structure, causing it to crack before allowing him to taste victory? Nelson's trainers had taught him to use the pole in a certain special way. The strength and agility required to accomplish these jumps were surely worthy a gold medal. Nelson had also discovered a way to reach even higher than the highest point allowed by the normal hands' grip position by simply "walking" with his hands as if his arms were legs instead. Also called "step walking . . ." as if using a ladder on the uppermost section of the pole, and by practically standing on one hand at the very top of the vault, Nelson could push his body in a straight-up position, feet first, and then by bending over and above he was able to drop onto the other side of the vault's high bar barrier that forms the threshold between victory and defeat! Nelson's luck during the last few days had not been as tremendous as he might have wished. Still, he harbored no doubts that by selectively applying his training he could become the gold medal winner in this activity.

The third ranking athlete opened the day's competitions. His score went up several points. The second man on the general classification followed next, displaying a superb combination of agility and coordination. Although on his second trial he had scored lower than during the first, on the third one, he surpassed his best effort ever! With it he had not only shattered the Olympic record—but his performance had created a problem for Nelson St★.

The spectators who had been warming up enthusiastically with these two first competitors' exhibition of mastery reached a frenzy at the flashing of the news indicating which competitor was coming up next. And in unison, before the spectators' applause had subsided, the name "Nelson! Nelson! Nelson!" was being chanted and heard from every angle. Nelson's sudden appearance in the green zone drove the crowds crazy. Calmly though, he prepared for his first trial after graciously having acknowledged the fans' magnificent tribute, and their spontaneous recognition.

Standing with the pole in his hands, concentrating on his jump, Nelson reviewed in his mind the advice of his trainers. The crowd grew quiet. The announcement of his turn then came on the loud speaker once again. After another short burst of applause, silence reigned all around, interrupted only by sporadic coughing and by the disturbing but perhaps inadvertent "calling" of some competitors' names by their loving but otherwise poor-mannered fans. It was followed then, out of respect at observing Nelson's body language, by the most beautiful, impressive, unforgettable moment of absolute stillness. Invoking the names of the Olympian gods while addressing the heavens with a concentrated mind and a lifted spirit reflected on his face, Nelson implored victory through the souls of the Olympian champions of the past, with eyes closed momentarily to give emphasis to his prayer, and then he ran down the path with a powerful sprint, totally assured of himself. Wobbling while in motion the pole's front end hit the ground at the precise point in the "V" shape box, bending in a semi circular manner while catapulting Nelson all the way up. His body shot ahead . . . on a straight line . . . reaching the top. The spectators, glued to his spectacular performance, were still totally silent; the judges, very aware. But before Nelson could swing over to the other side of the cross bar, and catching the astonished spectators by surprise, his pole, which had already reached the breaking point moments earlier, gave way . . . and brought Nelson back down with all his body's weight to the same side of the path. Screeching with terror and anxiety, the surprised audience panicked. Horrified and concerned, the crowd saw Nelson dropping from an altitude of about twenty-two feet down to the bare floor. A moment of confusion took hold of everyone in the stadium. The emergency medical crew rushed over to the site. The next few but eternally long seconds were completely filled with total silence and some consternation, emptying the entire atmosphere of any enthusiasm felt up to now. Sobbing was then heard from different sections in the stadium. The medics and the Olympic officials were busy trying to make a decision. For a few interminably long minutes no one knew what to expect; what to say; or what to do.

Then, in the middle of the suspense produced by his unexpected fall, Nelson St★ got up. The crowd hesitated. He moved around stretching his arms and legs. The fans, at this excruciating point, unable to contain their happiness and repressed emotions, burst into applause and cheers. Nelson bowed in every direction in the stadium toward that spectacular public, in recognition of their affection, and proceeded to regain his position in order to repeat his jump. This time the crowd kept on cheering furiously and applauding louder and louder, giving encouragement to their "fallen idol!"

Nelson then, with calculated decision, having obtained a new pole, ran the stretch of the track, and with a powerful push lifted himself up, higher than before. "Walking" with his hands on the upper portion of the pole as his instructors had taught him earlier, he reached the top, soaring like an eagle to a height never achieved before by any other Olympic athlete and, bending swiftly over and above the obstacle bar, he fell gently onto the landing cushion on the other side . . . as an angel in flight descending from heaven.

The fans were ecstatic. They simply went crazy. Their feelings were expressed once again—longer this time—by giving Nelson St★ his well-deserved "crown" of applause. After a few moments basking in the warm but momentary rays of his glory, bowing again to the multitude in recognition of their admiration, Nelson retired to his section to await the next competition. One more triumph had been achieved; one more gold medal had been earned by his prowess at this time. A triumph and a medal which Nelson offered to the Olympian gods, but which he believed belonged to his fans. Not too long after however, he was summoned again to the field of action. This time, for the Shot Put competition instead.

The Shot Put is one of those sports that requires a tremendous amount of technique, besides a very strong physique. Nelson demonstrated his ability in his first attempt when he threw the "iron ball" with such an elevation that it landed well beyond all his previous demarcations. It was not his best shot ever though! The crowd nevertheless was pleased and Nelson's name was repeatedly chanted by several groups alternating their praise.

The second athlete who competed performed then an unexpected feat. He matched Nelson's distance to the centimeter, keeping the score at the same level for this competition. The third man was even better. He sent the "put" soaring high into the skies and landing far beyond Nelson's mark. On his second attempt however, he went down too far, allowing Nelson a chance to improve his score. And that, he did! However, once again the number two athlete scored higher.

The crowd, in its eagerness to unbiasedly support all concerned, seemed to have been divided by then. Both athletes were, however, given the encouragement they deserved. Nelson had but one more throw—to either win or to lose. Not having anyone else on this Earth he could count upon to help him, he reached again to the Olympian gods! For a moment Nelson felt his aspirations were being shattered. The number two ranking competitor needed only to have scored the same as he to deprive him of the golden moment. And the least weakness on Nelson's part would automatically mean the silver medal instead. But perhaps his prayers would still be answered! Allowing himself a few extra seconds to gather all his mental and physical energies into a pool of strength . . . Nelson, in his last attempt, went over and beyond his first mark, culminating the event with a superb throw that surpassed even his own expectations. The fans knew it instantly. Without waiting for the official results, their resonant applause gave Nelson the triumph.

He bowed, thanking them in recognition of their accolade, and then retired to his training section. The second and third competitors had also finished with very high scores, but still under Nelson's total. Nelson's overall supremacy was reinstated with this event, and his dreams had been brought one step closer to the final victory! His was a truly magnificent triumph, a moment of success Nelson really needed not only to assert his domination over the field of talented competitors but mainly to secure his state of mind. Honors then were presented, as stipulated by the agreement between Nelson St★ and the I.O.C.

The transition between sports competitions allows the athletes some time to gather their thoughts and to recuperate part of their energy. During these transitions the athlete has the chance to mentally review the charts with the records already established; to relax peacefully, if not quietly; to get a massage; and/or mentally and emotionally prepare for the next performance. For Nelson, however, it was a moment to reconnect instead with the Olympian gods who so far had given him not only the chance to perform but the means to achieve. Achieving: that was exactly what Nelson expected to do in his next performance.

The Javelin represents hunting (. . . from the native peoples of the world). At war (. . . through the warriors in forgotten battles), and during competition (. . . to the athletes in international contests), the javelin has been a pathway for the natural expression of man's instincts, and a means to achieve a goal.

When we think of the human being in his primitive stage trying to survive the inclemencies of an unknown world, we think of caves; we think of fire; we think of food and clothes, and of the animals that supply both, meat and furs. Each step taken by this primitive human being in order to stay alive, brought a new development into his existence. The caves became houses; the fire, electricity. The furs (which belong exclusively to wild animals), and which in the long run became today's clothes, had to be obtained by developing at about the same time the tools to obtain, primarily, the food. The spear, the hunting lance (later on evolved into a more useful and even elegant weapon . . ., the so-called javelin) which came then into existence. An elaborate stick, actually, with a sharp end brought to precise length and weight, it has also been given its perfect balance. And when strength and durability were a minimum requirement for constant use and abuse, humans selected the strongest wood from among all the trees in the forest. Macana for instance, as the ancient Peruvian and Mexican Indians did, adding just a sharp flint to make it into a deadly weapon. Ebony, the black wood used in lieu of ivory (nature and animal; the latter protected by the first . . .). And the noble oak, and the mahogany tree! The perennial olive, whose leathery leaves, shaped as a "lance," festoons the rapturous heads of the crowned champions with their silvery undersides! All these among others, as the source from which to mold the best weapon to meet the needs of those who became professionals in the art of war and/or hunting!

Have you ever been deep into the jungle (the so-called "manigua"), visiting any tribe of Indians living in the impenetrable sections of the thick forest; have you ever roamed the desert where constantly moving caravans form the domain of the nomads; have you ever climbed a steep mountain to find a native dwelling among the clouds? If you have, you have rarely seen aborigines of distinction and/or social rank, (patriarchs mainly), without a "walking stick" as either the body's support—especially if the individual is of mature age—or as a companion weapon. Heir to a kind of a symbol invented by someone—nobody knows who, where or when—the person who employs it as part of daily life is usually the one who shows self assurance. And in the same manner it enhances personality, that same stick is used to provide for sustenance as well as for self defense. Even the scepter, that prestigious symbol among the princes of the world, has its origins in the humble stick of wood whence our javelin originally came. For those in a position of religious authority, the simple spear; the javelin; the lance; have been disguised as the "staff," and have become a symbol of supremacy, having the connotations of divine power stamped all over them, among some peoples of the world. Of course, that wooden stick is no other than the reproduction of the "caduceus" (snake staff . . .) that the Olympian god Mercury (originally known as Hermes . . .), the messenger of the gods, used as his own wand. The same stick that developed through the ages and through many different phases, into today's flagstaff, carrier of the symbol of glory and independence for every free nation; into the common conductor's rod; and into the tube carried and passed on by the runners in a relay race. The long stick carried and twirled by a drum major; a truncheon, a short club or cudgel carried by a gendarme; a Field Marshal's baton, etc., carrying in its "assorted changes" a certain degenerating *"je ne sais quoi!"* Something similar to the so-called "bathos," if the comparison in terminology could in this instance be accepted. (Like when a commonplace feature offsets an otherwise sublime situation.)

In the organized armies of the Greeks, and of the Romans, to mention just a couple of civilizations with preeminence in our history books, millions were killed in hand-to-hand combat. Arrows penetrated shields and wounded many soldiers. But spears formed the strength of the entire legion when they were used as weapons of specialized units. The phalanx, the war tanks of back then, handled by Greek warriors attacking in contingents the bulk of other armies. A bulwark, described by the Romans as "The Turtle." A group of soldiers "encaged" by their shields, displayed as a monster of flesh, leather and steel traversing swiftly like a serene, deep river with the devastating strength of a sea of men in constant movement during the fierce battles against torrents of marauders flooding the homeland. Yes—the war tanks we use today, were then, figuratively speaking, squads of warriors sometimes put together as whole companies, perhaps even as an entire legion (or as a large part of one, depending upon the space available to maneuver in the battle field) stitched together using longer lances like needles protruding from their shields . . . farther even than the length of today's javelins.

History is full of anecdotes describing the use of the lance as the appropriate weapon either for defense, or for attack. It was also considered as the favorite "arm," (or as an extension of the arm) in knightly duels during the medieval age, as well as the most useful and resourceful weapon used by the Crusaders. The spear was used as a gladiator's tool in the arena. And the javelin, you might say, actually became such when either the spear or the lance were thrown through the air trying to reach, not only the beast who was being hunted, but the approaching enemy, as well as a fleeing adversary during a cavalry regiment's attack. Nations still motivate brigades of soldiers on horse to prepare for duty in a specialized force where the training includes the use of the javelin, the spear (or more accurately, the lance) mainly as an honorary guard corps, name that still today properly identifies its fighting military unit.

The Olympics have forced upon our society a preconceived idea of what this particular sport is all about. However, some peoples around the world have used the "javelin" displayed in other forms to create a symbol of their national cultural enterprises. They have developed the use of the lance in so many different forms in their martial arts sciences, for instance, that it is almost impossible to distinguish their ways from the original manner in which the same kind of spear was used by aborigines in other lands, in their own special circumstances. Dexterity seems to be the only quality that separates the cultures.

Many nations have their own permanent teams of athletes representing almost every known sport. Some nations restrict their athletic world to only a few types of sports, but must include the main events that usually form part of the decathlon, just in case those same athletes become one day part of the group that might be able to participate in any future Olympian competition. It is well known that in modern times the javelin has always been one of the main classical sports practiced today. Dexterity on the javelin is still highly esteemed, and the javelin is highly regarded as a means to achieve. . . .

This sport has continually fascinated humans with an adventurous spirit. As far as Nelson was concerned, it represented one of the classic expressions of the Greek era so well emulated by the Romans, copied by their conquered warriors and their subdued armies, and brought to a "golden age" by soldiers from armed forces representing all the ethnic groups from every nation on this Earth.

This third event of the second day of the decathlon was certainly a sport for spectators to enjoy. If other sports require strength, speed, and stamina, the javelin demands graceful precision as well. Making a lance fly with rhythm is not an easy task. Aerodynamics are instinctively applied by those who conscientiously devote time and effort to pursue it. The results have always proved the theory.

Among this game's competitors were three whose records proved to be the best in the globe. First, the holder of the Olympic title. Second, the champion of the world. And third, a national hero. All three were eager to accept new challenges and to improve on their performance.

It was early in the afternoon. The sun was shining with unusual strength. Its brilliant rays pelted fans seated in the bleachers, burning them inclemently. The competition started with an extraordinary performance by the national champion, whose new score broke his own national mark and brought him up some points in the total average. The Olympic champion followed. With his throw, a new record was also established. The public could not believe the spectacle they were witnessing. Their enthusiasm was high. When the world champion's turn came about, the fans showered him with incredibly strong and long applause. Nelson was pleased that the crowd was so fervent. After this young man's demonstration of professional ability, all records, the Olympic, the national and the world championship, had been once again, totally shattered.

It was now Nelson St★'s chance to prove himself against the best there had ever been. . . . Once again Nelson came out on the green zone. Instantaneously, the multitude received him with the most spontaneous demonstration of affection. Shouting and whistling, the fans saluted Nelson for a long, long while. . . . After taking his time selecting his spear, Nelson finally went to the starting position. Raising the javelin to the level of his head with a half-way stretched-out arm, he paused for a few seconds to concentrate on his next step. The expectation had grown thick at all corners of the stadium. Among the fans, not even a whisper was overheard. There was no movement. The wind, swiftly blowing moments earlier between the stadium floor and the high roof, in an unsuccessful attempt to escape, ceased its susurrus to allow Nelson the concentration he required!

That wind, as if following the path of an invisible, open spiral staircase given physical form by the dust and by the debris blown off and being carried up in the way a whirlwind toys with the sweepings in an open field—that wind, suddenly, ceased to exist. The judges looked on with cautious eyes ready to inscribe yet another triumph. Again, Nelson hesitated. He brought his lance down. The spectators were given the impression that Nelson was not going to be able to compete. A soft sigh of disappointment was then heard throughout. On the big board an electronic sign apologized for the momentary inconvenience. A round of applause, the nervous expression of some frustrated fans, followed. Then, Nelson requested that he be allowed to exchange his lance for another longer and heavier one, which he had brought along as part of his training kit. Although still under regulation, this new javelin had never been used during competition, but Nelson felt comfortable with it.

A few minutes passed. The public was noticeably anxious. At last Nelson went back to the starting position where a soft wind was now in his favor. Raising again his spear, he thrust forward with every bit of energy in his body. Then, with the precision of a great athlete he sent his javelin flying high and long . . . to land smoothly and securely at a point half way between the markers of the holders of the Olympic and of the world records.

The spectators cheered. Quietly then, Nelson walked away to await his chance for a second attempt. On his second throw he was even better. With it, the world's record was also broken. The crowd then became ecstatic. One more try, and Nelson would surely finish the competition as a winner. Several minutes passed. Chanting his name, the public demanded of him to perform. Willing to please everyone, Nelson took the javelin for a third and a last try. Kneeling with his left leg only, he set the lance across his thigh. He closed his eyes. Then, mentally and spiritually . . . Nelson seemed to pray. Everyone fell silent. Not even a breath was heard from the crowd. TV announcers reported that viewers all over the world were fascinated by this unusual fifty-year-old competitor, and that fan clubs had started to form in many large cities in order to honor Nelson St★.

The spectators were temporarily restraining themselves (some being held back by security personnel) within their own sections, awaiting the results of the final show of prowess during the last attempt at this sport, by this extraordinary athlete.

At last the moment of truth arrived. Slowly, Nelson got up and, walking with pride, returned to the starting point. Seconds passed during which only the murmur of his heart interrupted the stillness in the air. After he had taken his position, and with all the determination of a hero in the making, Nelson sprinted forward with all his might carrying his javelin high above his head. Just before he reached the spot from which he had to hurl his spear, he first balanced his step. With a swing that employed every muscle in his body, he had his right arm stretched out backward and all the way low to its maximum position. At the same time, he balanced himself out with his left arm raised forward and high, forming the figure of an eagle in flight and, with an instinctive propulsive move to be able to thrust forward, he flung the javelin up into the blue skies farther and higher than he had ever done it before. (Metaphorically speaking, through the heavens went flying the lances thrown by a thousand warriors, battling an army of demigods.) Piercing the skies under that firmament already wounded by spears destined for humanity, Nelson's javelin crossed the distances expertly traveled by millions of arrows during earlier wars. The arrows of the archers from the armies that had conquered the ancient world that time lost; that world in which warriors were defeated in battles many a time, but where wars have always been won. Fortunately, indeed, for Nelson St★ personally, another such challenge had just simply been overcome; would he, at the end, still win likewise his own war?

The fans didn't know how to express their admiration. Many behaved—unfortunately—in the crude way they were accustomed to whenever they went to a similar kind of spectacle at home. Barriers were broken. Runners disturbed many spectators. But some jumpers and some runners who wanted to go down to the green lawn in demonstration of their personal feelings, were this time caught by security personnel. Some not even caring about their actions, while others not fully realizing that with such enthusiasm and behavior they were simply disruptive to all. Nelson St★'s heroism had once again conquered the hearts of the public who in turn showed its fervor with long and thunderous applause. His last try had given him not only a higher point average in the general score, but had won him a new world record in this sport. Golden was indeed the moment cherished by one and all on that brilliantly lit sunny afternoon in that magnificent stadium filled with avid sports fans from around the globe (and who knows, from other parts of the galaxy, perhaps). After this triumph for Nelson St★, he was required to think ahead to the next event—the discus throw, a precision type of event that was yet to come.

(*Ah! The classic Discus competition that was still to come!*)

The *Discus* was the favorite sport of Nelson St★. Yes, certainly. Embedded in Nelson's mind he had always carried the image of the Greek Olympic champion suspended in the middle of his swing at the moment of hurling the Discus. (That unknown champion, possibly named "Diskos" circa 400 B.C., so well depicted by Myron in his bronze statue of the Discus Thrower). Nelson had frequently fantasized about exceeding all expectations during his performance of this classic sport, and he had often transported himself mentally to the origins of the Olympics, where he had found a niche for himself among the Greek players. For him, along with the Javelin throw and the exhausting Hurdles, this event symbolized the epitome of the Olympic Games.

For Nelson, each competition represented something special to the Greeks who wanted to celebrate with each sport every individual aspect of their lives.

Nelson rationalized every one of the sports of the Olympic Games as a way to relive the episodes of war, fought in hand to hand combat by the meticulously trained, well organized armies of the Greeks, the Romans, and other ancient peoples who followed their lead; civilizations whose lives depended on the triumphs of their soldiers on the battlefield, and to thank Motherland for providing them with the abundant and adequate natural resources and economic means. To Nelson's mind, the following are a few of these classic sports that still form part of the modern Olympics. *Sprint:* To deliver war messages at the earliest possible time, before the enemy had the opportunity either to retreat or to regroup. *Marathon:* The long, forced, exhausting marches to meet the enemy at the most strategic location, and at the most convenient time. *Wrestling and Fencing:* The actual hand to hand combat. *The High* and the *Long Jumps:* The ups and downs, crossing the new territories with their war matériel toward distant fields of battle. *The Pole Vault:* A remembrance of the obstacles conquered over gorges and rivers when warriors had to jump across to reach their final destination. *The Shot Put:* The catapult's throwing of the "bullets of fire" over their enemy's military camps' stockade fences, and over the fortified stone walls into their towns, as well as from ship to ship over calmed waters concealing the abyssal burial ground from previous encounters during battles fought at sea. *The Javelin:* The actual flying of the lancers' spears, and of the archers' arrows, searching to pierce the enemy soldiers' shields and to embed themselves deeply into their hearts during the skirmishes of war. *And the Discus! Ah! The Discus!* Soaring high like a bird of prey to deliver a war's declaration, or cruising swiftly as a carrier pigeon to bring a message of temporary peace won by the spilling of blood from human lives!

Nelson came in third on his first discus throw. He scored second on his next try. And, by Apollo! He defeated his opponents in his last attempt. He did not believe it at first, but then!!!

Having pulled all his energies together and with the determination of a real champion, Nelson pivoted on the throwing circle, and hurled into the skies the message he had always wanted to send to the entire universe in the form and the shape of the discus!

In its flight, this time it was not the allegoric "white dove" carrying a message of peace. The strength and fury of the throw was more like a reminder of the bird of prey which, descending upon the enemy at a speed that seemed to match the velocity of light, was bringing with it a challenge of total war to every other contender in the field. A war where the mind is strategically evaluating the battles to determine their final outcome; a war where the soul abuses its attributes to make legal their moral overtones—and a war where the body, in conjunction with the mind and the soul, brings together the efforts of the athlete to win over the challenge when the opponent must finally give up. For Nelson St★, winning another battle was important at this stage of the Games, of course. However, in this case it was mainly a battle against himself. Nevertheless, the overall result with the final victory is what everyone is always looking for in any competition played to be won.

What a sublime instant it was! At the moment of his throwing the discus, in the minds of the spectators it was not the physical person of Nelson St★, the individual, they were admiring most. No—as if superimposed by a Power with supernatural abilities beyond human understanding (and observed through the eyes of the mystery woman whose face was already familiar to Nelson), it was instead the real athlete, who, millennia ago, had performed his prowess in front of the Greek crowds congregated for the first Olympian games with powerful muscles that proclaimed him a latter-day Hercules, Nelson St★, in a flash, appeared to the spectators as a vision from Mount Olympus, Heaven on Earth for the Olympian gods! No one in that stadium understood; they simply accepted the phenomenon without the ability to question it. They saw Nelson **transmogrified**, playing the role of the first winner of the first Olympic Games, surrounded by all the deities paying homage to the new champion. A wreath of olive flowers adorned his head, emblematic of his victory; the flash—momentary at best—then faded away!

The crowd went wild. Subconsciously moved by such a glimpse at an "eternal moment" of the past, and overwhelmed by Nelson's deeds, spectators hyped with passionate fervor by the announcement over the electronic board, responded with an incredible standing ovation. "Gold!" "Gold!" "Gold!" they chanted repeatedly, melting their hearts into twenty-four karats of genuine enthusiasm! Thus ended then the discus event, Nelson's personally considered classic sport of the Olympics, and the one of his own predilection.

And with this fade-out, only one competition remained. *Just one more battle to be fought.* One more triumph for Nelson to achieve; one more possibility of partial victory, with which to win, at the end, the total war.

The 1500 Meters. Reminiscent of the forced marches into foreign lands, where distant locations had to be reached—locations where sometimes you could only get to, after agonizing and exhausting effort, for weeks at a time, in order to conduct an offensive as well as a defensive military campaign. And then came those marches in reverse, the return home not just from having won a bloody battle by defeating brave opponents, determined warriors, and noble enemies, but from successfully achieving peace with a complete victory that had been obtained only at the completion of a devastating war. The triumphal march, the parade along with one's military peers to be proudly crowned a hero among your friends, your fans, and your loved ones. That is what the 1500 Meters event supposedly represented for Nelson St★ when in retrospect he considered the skirmishes of war a means to conquer other lands; and in doing so, the proliferation of one culture, in order to enhance—or to destroy—another world!

Among most decathlon competitors there is a certain fear about the 1500 Meter competition because it demands speed and endurance at the same time. These two elements are well known to take a toll out of every athlete contending in the Olympics, as well as in any other sports competition (national or international). The rate of performance imposes a limit of maximum work to minimum time spent ratio. And the capacity of bearing up during prolonged stress is forced upon the contender, not only by other athletes participating in the same event, but by factors of the participant's own personality, nationality, ethnic background and economic situation. And when it is scheduled as the last event of the decathlon, it becomes an added hazard that usually will subtract from the final score. Exhausted by waiting and by the rigors of competing, all athletes are by then almost totally depleted. Nevertheless, everyone still gives their best.

Some, better than average in this kind of sport, and who consider it their best chance to increase their final score, will conserve their energies for this climactic event until the very end, in order to emerge strongly enough to turn low marks into achievements, previous defeats into victory.

Athletes number five and number six on the general classification were both world champion runners of the 1500 Meter event. Although they were not a threat to Nelson St★ to become the winner of the decathlon at the end of this competition, this last link in the golden chain of Olympic medals won by Nelson so far, was at stake nevertheless. Before this event, the public had practically crowned Nelson already as their champion. How could he disappoint his fans now, at the last moment? And—more importantly—would he disappoint himself at this point and time in the Games?

It was late in the afternoon. Over five hours had already passed since the opening of the stadium gates for the first competition of the day. The public was still on edge, however, and preparations for the 1500 Meter race were well under way. Excitement still reigned throughout the Olympic Stadium. Although aware that he should try to remain calm, Nelson St★ could not relax. In his mind weighed the responsibility of achieving the final victory. Not that he had any doubts about winning at the end, given this particular event's classification. No, that was not the case; it was just one of those times and circumstances during which every athlete is concerned with the remote possibility of failure, and feels on the down side. Nelson's ruminations were almost palpable. *What if I lose my position instead, by losing this competition? Then what? What will happen if I cannot score a high mark? If I should lose too many points, and consequently, I do not win the decathlon at the end either?* What a wounding, pessimistic viewpoint. Why has this suddenly surfaced, just after so many triumphs in such a short time? Who knows? Perhaps he would never understand. . . . But it's only natural. It happens to many athletes just before they start a competition. *My athletic integrity would be compromised though if I didn't do my best, to say the least?* And this thought gave him the answer he really needed, the answer he was looking for. So, he decided instinctively that he would do his best, as he had always done! That's right. That was all he could do, his best! And with this thought, and the ensuing decision, Nelson's deep psychological "wound" was immediately healed! And while mentally and emotionally he prepared himself for the 1500 Meters event, luckily enough, the spectators had calmed down from the excitement of the previous competition, offering him a little bit of peace. Some public agitation, however, could still be sensed all around as they waited for the preparations for the last of the decathlon events to be finished, and for the new spectacle to begin.

It was a beautiful afternoon indeed. Partially sunny skies, peppered with some dark clouds navigating the heavens, reflected Nelson's feelings. It was as if his soul, his mind, the sunny side of his reasoning was wide open to triumph, but some unidentifiable, somber feeling clouded his thinking. In general, the vast extent of blue firmament sprinkled with light from the sun shining obliquely from above, emphasized instead his clear thoughts about the events to follow.

The name of Nelson, and his picture, were constantly being flashed on the electronic board. At each instance the fans went crazy. For the public in the stadium, Nelson St★ was now deified. All the other athletes were given their deserved honors with long applause whenever their names were mentioned—but only Nelson received an ovation every time. Was it a request by the public? Or was it, perhaps, a demand? Nelson had once said (and the media never let him forget it): "Idols must satisfy their iconoclastic subjects in order to maintain their place on the pedestal of glory!" But "glory," per se (meaning "honoring posthumously with eternal memory"), meant absolutely nothing to him. Nelson had also posited that glory was achieved only by superior men. But, like everything transitory, glory can become a wreath of dried-out petals oppressing the temples of a noble head! Fans' ideals transform ordinary men into their own idols; then, the fans demand their real idols' glory for themselves—but if unable to obtain it, they try to impose.

Deep in Nelson's soul everything was now clarified. No doubts about himself or about his performance existed. Consequently, for Nelson St ★, the gratification of the public was irrelevant, however pleasing.

But, doing his best? Aha! That was his *duty!* Nelson knew that integrity of character is the mother of all virtues. Of that he was well aware. And he used that motto not only in interpersonal situations, but to rule his life as an athlete. Nelson had not forgotten the days of his youth when a Utopian Olympics was the extent of his ability to compete. Neither had forgotten his moments of inertia, loneliness and depression, suffered after the accident that decimated his family. But these were different times now. To preserve all that was precious to him, and for himself, he had to win again! And as far as the crowd was concerned, the effervescence of the moment during those ovations produced the emotional bubbles that started to blow up, like stunning fireworks, bringing the decathlon competition to a festive culmination.

All the competitors were at last lined up. The gun shot announcing the start of the final event resounded like thunder throughout the Olympic Stadium. The long silence that had preceded this inaugural episode was instantly broken, and was then immediately followed by the most fervent demonstration of sports fever ever recorded for posterity.

A group of seven competitors took to the front instantly. Streamlining after the first turn, all remained close to one another. Among them Nelson St★ kept his place, some moments as the fourth runner, some others as the sixth. The fans' enthusiastic shouting encouraged Nelson not to give up but to move forward instead.

Toward the end of the second turn everyone was still holding together as a pack. The spectators kept yelling with emotion. (Each fan of course, had selected already his/her favorite runner.) But by now, Nelson had commanded the attention of every body present in the stadium. Besides, the world's television viewers at home, who had been monitored from the beginning of the decathlon, were perceived as being eagerly supportive now of that fifty-year-young, "incredible" human being.

Half way into the competition, two runners from the front group were lagging about twenty feet behind, exhausted by their efforts during the first minutes of the race. The pace had been unbelievably fast, but oddly, Nelson did not seem to be tired at all. The two world champions; an Olympic marathon winner; and a two-time champion of the 10,000 meter try-outs from previous years, remained in front, along with Nelson St★. What was keeping Nelson going alongside such powerful competitors? Something more than good training and determination? Of course!

It was noted by some spectators during the race (and confirmed afterwards), that some fans could have sworn to have seen Nelson St★ competing without even touching the ground when certain moves were made by the front runners. How was that possible? Was that the reason for the public's excessive enthusiasm? Were the fans being manipulated, perhaps, by some other special telepathic energy floating in the air? Nelson's name had been hysterically chanted from the beginning of the competition, but that was seen as a normal behavior. But then, in response perhaps to his move and as if cued by it, when Nelson advanced swiftly to the front, taking position number two toward the end of this event, the fans started instead to break the barriers separating the spectator sections and to jump down the steps toward the green lawn. Security guards and police were instantly mobilized to protect not only those persons who were acting with such fervor, but mainly all the athletes who were still competing. In the time it took the runners to complete the remaining turn around the green zone, hundreds of admirers had invaded the "sacred grounds" of the Olympic sports competition. The unrestrained enthusiasts had dropped down onto the running tracks and had literally taken possession of the Olympic arena. Fortunately however, these irrationally behaving spectators had—coincidentally—arrived at just about the same time that the competition was ending with the incredible, unbelievable victory of Nelson St★. Exerting great effort at the last moment and with a powerful thrust, as if propelled by the force emanating from a steam engine attached to his feet, Nelson crossed the finish line ahead of all his brave and fast competitors. His triumph then, in the middle of the multitude gathered already at the finish line, became at the same time the celebration all spectators craved from the beginning of that glorious second day of Olympic history.

The ovation grew louder and longer, reaching frenzy at the end of that last golden moment when Nelson was finally announced as the winner of the decathlon. The crowd was at this point completely out of control. Raising Nelson upon their shoulders, and sliding him over from side to side as if he was floating over the waves of a sea in movement, fans from every nation congregated now as one group carrying their new Olympic champion; their newest Olympic god; and the hero of the moment.

With Nelson's victory announced through the loud-speakers, chaos reigned over the Olympic Village. Never in the history of the Games had a single athlete commanded such a following!

Three times around the tracks under the most unbelievably fervent demonstration of love and admiration, manifested by the chanting of "Nelson! Nelson! Nelson!", and by the warmest of ovations, didn't seem to be enough tribute to be given to this new hero who had so gallantly exhibited not only courage and strength, but integrity, from beginning to end.

Scarcely able to control the friendly crowd of fans within the limits of the green zone, and strongly requesting of the rest of the public to remain in their own seats, the police were finally able to allow the athletes to be safely on their own. In view of the circumstances, and believing it to be a great honor, many of these athletes broke away from their own exercises and joined the celebration with great pleasure and joy. It was, indeed, the right thing to do for the heroic sports figure who had broken all records, and who had elevated himself to the highest pedestal in the history of the Games, uplifting along with him every athlete in that stadium and every individual whose honest intentions were to become someday just like Nelson St★, the true Golden Boy.

Still hearing the applause from the public, and in a manner already familiar to all his fans, Nelson St★ bowed in every direction several times. He then calmly, but suddenly and inexplicably left the stadium, oblivious to his promise to stand at attention when the anthem of the countries of the Silver and of the Bronze medal winners were to be played.

Although profound anxiety was felt by the fans when Nelson went away, the applause and the chanting of his name still persisted for quite a while, lasting a total of thirteen consecutive minutes. Instinctively, as in the human wave (or perhaps being commanded telepathically by an unknown force), such a prolonged ovation was carried out by individual sections of the stadium, one by one rising to the occasion, and done with spontaneity by each for some specific length of time, so that some people could rest their hands . . . while the honor continued! It was a magnificent, and spectacular moment of incredible beauty, to be cherished forever. Each side of the stadium, rising in sequence, as a puppet being lifted by a mysterious and invisible hand, contrasted with the opposite side, sitting at the end of their turn, and bringing to life in unison the beauty of the colors of their flags represented by their lustrous attires.

Then suddenly, a dispirited feeling, a totally devastating chill permeated the entire atmosphere when throughout the stadium a "person to person" message was passed along. The Master of Ceremonies confirmed seconds later through the loud speakers, that Nelson St★, the new Olympic "god" and their beloved "idol"; the "athlete of the century . . ." had actually, inexplicably, and mysteriously . . . *disappeared!!!*

Almost instantaneously, rumors circulated about a possible kidnapping. Throughout the stadium there were whispers that Nelson St★ was perhaps an extraterrestrial, with an "alien" connection. Tension increased. Speculation "explained" temporarily, Nelson's possible whereabouts. . . . Some accounts even indicated that several people had actually witnessed Nelson vanishing from their view. . . . *("He simply wasn't there any longer!")* Their testimony of course was considered irrational by everyone at that time. But Olympic officials could not immediately deny the public's allegations; neither could they account for Nelson's absence, or for the simultaneous disappearance of his helpers and trainers.

After hours of search, local, national and international police were placed on the alert, and squads of specialized members from the different branches of all the military forces were ordered to search for him. Authorities heard that terrorist groups had claimed his possession. Throughout the night, television and radio bulletins broadcasting news about Nelson's "fate" alarmed (but did not inform) the entire world. The Olympic Village became then a military parade ground.

The one member of Nelson's "team" who could be found, was Cynthia, who did not have any explanation to give anyway. However, remembering the mountain Nelson had aspired to conquer, she promised to look into the matter. Cynthia remembered that, on many stressful occasions (especially when he felt depressed, or at those moments when his thoughts carried him beyond the confines of this existence), Nelson would escalate again that mountain, searching for answers. After due consideration, Cynthia secretly telephoned her editor and suggested that he go along with the sheriff to the top of the butte, where Nelson just might be.

News of Nelson's "vanishing act" was blasted all over the entire world. Television viewers ratified the testimony of some of the fans who were present at the site, by reiterating what they had "seen" that afternoon!

In Nelson's hometown and in those other places he had visited before, when a child, the stunning news hit as an ice storm. Those who knew Nelson, aware of his incredible mental capacity paired now with his Olympic abilities, feared for him. Such unusual individuals do not come by the bunch—they are simply unique! Yes, indeed. The apprehension of possible crime was well justified. Nelson's extraordinary combination of brain acumen and athletic prowess would surely make an excellent bargaining chip for those unscrupulous whose métier was crime. The scientific community, as well as females searching for the perfect male to procreate the heir to their own intellectual, physical and/or economic fortunes, would be more than happy to fulfill their desires. Those who had only heard of Nelson, had by then become his fans and were now concerned for his well being. . . . A searching party that had been organized by Cynthia and her editor (who had been requested by her to secretly comb every step of "Nelson's mountain," as it became known, internationally, from that day on . . .), was unable to 'shine a light' onto any alien craft landing on any section of the territory, as it was expected. But after some time however, the inquisitive nature of the police and of the news media partially paid off. In the middle of an extensive patch surrounded by dry grass, on the other side of Nelson's mountain, away from the town's lights, among some ancient trees whose longest and most frondose branches had been broken, and whose top foliage had been badly burnt, a rare looking mark appeared to have been ironed on the surface of the ground. It had the shape of a disk with oval spots around it, buried almost two feet deep, like the trail left by a set of heavy leg-supporters holding an extremely large circular platform. This indicated to scientists that a metal object of large proportions, emanating abundant heat from its powerful energy, had left its ("fingerprints . . .?") own identifying set of tracks!!! What was it? Nobody knew. Perplexity invaded the minds of those who had witnessed the phenomenon. And as far as the police investigators and the scientists who later visited that location were concerned, they were unfortunately unable to locate any trace of Nelson, or to corroborate his reputed "alien" connection. When radiation tests were performed on the spot, not even a basic indication of any exceptional other-worldly findings was perceived. (Only the putative "trail diagram" impressed upon the ground.) Reporting back to the IOC (through Cynthia, of course, who, as a knowledgeable journalist wasn't about to reveal any compromising information without a "subject" to back up her story), the town's folks simply denied finding Nelson in the neighborhood. And the night ended with unanswered questions and unfulfilled expectations.

Some witnesses testified that before disappearing from the Olympic Village, Nelson and his companions had been overtaken . . . and detained . . . by members of the press who had held them momentarily, hoping for some answers to questions they didn't even know how to ask. What could that have meant? Were they really members of the press, or were they agents of doom instead, disguised as news media personnel? Knowing what was at stake—who knows? *Would anyone?* Along with Nelson and other athletes were of course the helpers and the trainers whom reporters have been trying for a long time to interview. After posing nonchalantly for photo opportunities, Nelson, obviously hoping to cover his tracks, had quickly introduced his companions before answering any compromising questions at that particular time. Even though all individuals concerned did answer the news people's barrage on different topics, technically speaking they did it simply and laconically, with no tell-tale inflection. The helpers/trainers ended their interview with a single dismissing sentence: "We'll all have our own stories to tell when the Games are over!"

However, during the hours lapsed between this interview and the special broadcast that had been scheduled to bring news of the official confirmation of Nelson's disappearance, the press members had enough time to try to investigate further the peoples' new idol and his unexplained vanishing act. The media had time also to get ready every single question they had previously prepared, which hopefully would be properly answered then, with enough detail, to put aside definitely all their doubts. Was this a compromising position for Nelson St★ which forced him to make a drastic decision at that precise moment?

On that same evening, some representatives from the news media had requested a press conference with the IOC members. But during this conference, some TV camera operators and press photographers brought to the attention of the IOC's authorities instead, the fact that "Neither the trainers, nor the helpers of Nelson St★, had 'registered' on their film and/or video tapes." Also, that among the previously taken photographs, which had been very carefully re-examined, "Some only showed a blurry image that in most cases was dismissed as the camera's lens being out of focus; as a defective video tape; and/or as a simple mistake made by the person who had taken the pictures. But that this time however," and so they insisted, "there was no error!" That . . . "They (the so-called aliens as rumors were spreading it . . .), simply did not register!!!"

Unable to do anything about the complaint brought by the photographers, and by the news media personnel, the IOC's representatives, along with the government officials, vigorously requested of the press that they postpone their investigation of such matters until after the Closing Ceremonies. They were more concerned with the safety of Nelson St★, of course, whose whereabouts were still totally unknown. Reluctantly, almost everyone agreed but, as was expected, there were several press services which, more concerned with making a profit at someone else's expense than with the safety of anyone involved, made public nevertheless their suspicions. And, to everyone's surprise, and up to a degree confirming many peoples' presentiments, during that night's television and radio newscasts, and followed in the next morning's newspapers columns, more rumors circulated that the "trainers" and the "helpers" who had been with Nelson St★ from the Olympics' onset, were actually **aliens**, and that Nelson St★ himself was, to put it succinctly, **"not even human!!!"**

11

The Closing Ceremonies were about to begin, under a clean, blue, gorgeous sky. A sunny morning. The sun was radiantly warming not just the bodies of every athlete and of every spectator, but every heart and soul inside of that . . . from now on . . . eternally known and remembered . . . Intergalactic Classic Olympic Stadium. The temperature was perfect! No person born and raised in any tropical country in the world, could complain about the weather. And no fan from any other country, above or below the line of the equator, could have asked for a better reading on the Fahrenheit scale. At 10:00 A.M. the stadium was already packed. In addition to the regular crowd of spectators, there was a special, very select, handpicked group of persons for each country on Earth represented in the Olympics, who had been sent by their own governments for this unique occasion, and specifically with the mission to show not only moral, but economic support as well, for Nelson St★.

What was, however, the most astonishing thing that ever happened in any event of this category throughout history, was the fact that all fans in the stadium had come back, this time purposefully, dressed in their national colors. They were sitting, intentionally, following the pattern of the flag of their own countries. They were displaying themselves, patriotically, like a human emblem, comprising each country's national symbol, in a repetition of the original design as it had been brilliantly exhibited for the very first time ever, on the second day of the decathlon.

What a magnificent spectacle! You could feel the adrenaline at every corner of the stadium, in every occupied seat, in every fan's demeanor, rushing up through the veins making every person tremble with enthusiasm and with pleasure. Then, that unique, very special moment was finally reached! A triumphant moment for everyone; a moment you can't really describe, a moment no one will ever forget . . . A moment experienced only once in a lifetime. You had to be there to believe it! All of a sudden, those pre-selected groups from among the spectators from all the represented nations spontaneously *started to sing*. And along with them, the entire world, those present at the stadium and on the air, the TV viewers, sang along. And between stanzas of their patriotic songs, which included not only their own national anthems (but also popularly accepted hymns with well known lyrics and martial compositions, and even some with religious connotations), the name "Nelson! Nelson! Nelson!" was chanted repeatedly with fervor and devotion. The public's passion, climbing the mountains made out of clouds of emotion, had rapidly escalated to the highest peak, step by step, as in a ladder going up toward the heavens. The fans had come not just to watch their idols one last time . . . but to give them love and to demonstrate appreciation and recognition for their prowess. And, wearing their colorful attires besides, these fans were not only representing their countries with pride, but were, certainly, manifesting the true meaning of their noblest of feelings.

Viewed from above, the Olympic Stadium looked like a tropical garden adorned with thousands of human flowers of different colors surrounding the large green field, which of itself resembled an emerald jewel "gift wrapped" with the brick red ribbon formed by the running track around it. And as in every garden . . . when pollen emanating from the flowers' stamens is spread by the wind, the fans' admiration for all those athletes was perceived as coming from their hearts, conveyed in musical staffs, and sent as a message with their hymns.

At the precise time scheduled to start the Closing Ceremonies, the IOC authorities took their respective places on the balcony decorated expressly for the occasion. A large-sized flag (besides the flag of the Olympic organization, and the flag of the host country)—a unique flag, imposing, magnificent, electronically designed and digitally enhanced to make it float in the way a cloth flag waves its colors in the air when the wind blows in a straight direction at the level of the staff, adorned the site where the VIPs were located. When fully displayed, it depicted in slow animation, a blue firmament impregnated with colors vividly describing the way the confines of the Earth might look to humans observing a brilliant sundown, and indicative of the variable light seen in the sky at the time day turns slowly into twilight; a blue firmament, completely filled with scintillating stars and with a solar system composed of thirteen planets, one of which, the smallest, behaves as a moon, moving in and out of orbit among the others. These thirteen planets floated around a first magnitude sun . . . as brilliant as a billion stars studded constellation. This idea had been the brain child of Nelson St★, who hoped to display the image of the heavens he had been carrying in the memory banks of his incredible mind for a very long, long time. The image Nelson wanted humanity to see, with which to ponder the wonders of the universe outside the spatial boundaries of Mother Earth.

So—the parade marking the Closing Ceremonies began, an artistic showstopper that lasted at least 25 minutes, showcasing the talents of carefully selected members from the Olympian teams, and guided by an international troupe of artists of renowned merit, organized around a special theme, which was to convey the idea of the time lapsed between the first Olympics in antiquity and the present one—at the same time that it introduced all the athletes into the stadium. The purpose was also to bring out for the public's entertainment, understanding and reflection, as a historic point in mind, an excellent demonstration of how our ancestral ideals had come to be, and how they have contributed to make our world so great—ideals inherited directly from the original principles of democracy, of freedom and of justice, made possible (sometimes unfortunately), only by the imposition of force.

It is well known to the civilized world that, with few exceptions in history, religious instances to say the least, the strength of every epoch has been determined by either intellectual or by military power. (Intelligence: the teacher of science and of virtue, begetter of wisdom. Military: war and conquest. A power sometimes constructively destructive. And sometimes, even, destructively constructive. . . . History shows that war and conquest have been humans' idiosyncratic ways to fulfill their destiny!) The choreography was simply spectacular! Groups of young men and women, athletes and artists, dressed up in the appropriate regional costumes from those countries that had left their legacy of knowledge in other nations, succeeded one another, dancing in front of the spectators, after symbolically coming out of the darkness—the Dark Ages—and into the spotlight (modern days . . .), on the open stage. This spectacle was followed by squads of warriors attired also in the typical uniforms of the Armed Forces from those times "gone by," representing here the world powers that had instead imposed their rule onto others, changing the geographic boundaries of the ancient territories and their economic outlook. Each group from every nationality was thus preceded and then followed by a squad of soldiers that was supposed to bring to mind the idea of how each group's own epoch of historic value had started, and when it had ended. Then these squads were followed by the next group from the succeeding nationality that happened to represent the times in history that came after the events produced by the previous Armed Forces' conflict that had imposed the new changes in the world and that had founded what exists today, both, as an intellectual as well as economic and as a geographic legacy.

These men and women symbolically entering history (appearing on the stage . . .), representing one generation at a time, welcomed each then the following generation, bringing the idea of continuity in life, with the advances we enjoy today, and showing (when they exit the stage and go back into the dark again . . .), their passing through the ages as the centuries have flown by . . . over the same Earth that still remains. Following each squad of warriors representing the powerful nations that imposed change by war and conquest, the representatives of the best exponents of science and virtue, men and women who have constituted the essence of humanity, at intervals, in the history of this Earth, were also brought to light (onto the stage . . .). Alexander the Great. Gaius Julius Cæsar. Napoleon Bonaparte. Cristoforo Colombo. Confucius. Socrates. Jesus Christ. Mohammed. Albert Einstein—names that were exhibited in large characters for every spectator to see. The colorful uniforms in which all the young Olympians were dressed, and the special costumes with which they were clad, symbolizing their own nationalities, contrasted perfectly with the lush green color of the lawn in the center of the field. It was truly a brilliant kaleidoscopic, soothing scene, of human beauty!

It must, of course, be understood that at this time all nations' athletes were being honored. However, the official representatives of the Olympics, as well as the government authorities, had not yet been able to locate the whereabouts of Nelson St★, though they were still searching for him. In spite of the worries some athletes reflected on their faces and in their attitudes, one by one, always proudly (even majestically at times), every nation's group of contenders marched by the reviewing stand exhibiting the special glow that always accompanies a winning moment!

After all the participants had taken their place on the green zone, just about one hour or so into the ceremonies, all eyes were fixed on a specially selected group of people, a special committee presided by the Secretary of the United Nations, who had arrived specifically to present official greetings from the President of the country (who was also at hand), and very appropriately besides, the greetings and congratulations from the United Nations itself, along with several special medals of honor destined exclusively for Nelson St★. The President, the UN Secretary and the members of the Special Committee, had all come to bestow upon this hero, the "Citizenship of the Universe." In addition, a total of thirteen Honorary Doctorate Degrees from many national and foreign institutions, matching the number of languages Nelson could speak fluently. Nelson was recognized also as an asset for those same countries that had ironically denied him, prior to the Olympics, the honor of representing them. These emissaries had been sent to these proceedings with the sole purpose of carrying an open offer from their governments to give Nelson St★ the necessary economic means for a life with every comfort, and with the power to grant him any wish his heart desired for the rest of his existence on this Earth!

Still under the glitter displayed at the parade during the Opening Ceremonies, but only after the speeches from some important personalities had honored every athlete present and past, **Nelson St★** (*the idol of the multitudes, and the athlete of the year in the mind of every spectator*) **suddenly . . . and miraculously . . . presented himself again on this Earth!!!** The people who had personally witnessed the Olympic events on the stadium's grounds, plus those fans who had visually, mentally and emotionally accompanied Nelson while observing and enjoying the Games on television and radio, were treated to the most unforgettable moment in their lives. After having contemplated a universal SOS from the Olympic Committee imploring his immediate return, seconded by most governments from the planet, Nelson reappeared at the stadium's gates and went straightforward immediately onto the tracks inside that stadium . . . in the middle of a most thunderous ovation from the crowd congregated for the final stage of the Olympic competition. He was escorted by an impressive squad comprised of his trainers and helpers representing an elite unit of thirteen officers, from the lowest to the highest rank. These thirteen officers, resplendent in their magnificent festive uniforms, had the look of the classic type of the Greco/Roman soldiers resembling the ancient Prætorian Forces from the Roman Imperial Guard, known to have been founded by Cæsar Augustus.

Nelson and his cohort then started running at a slow pace, going around the tracks three times (which in itself constituted a triumphant march), in order to satisfy the public demand. The crowd—those loving fans he could now call his followers—somehow knew in advance (telepathically, perhaps?), that Nelson would return. . . . But when? That was the question. The world was obviously so sure that Nelson would reappear that multitudes went to the stadium well prepared to bestow upon him a gift rarely tendered any other athlete before. They were ready to give Nelson St★ their hearts, and let him take them into the recondite labyrinths of space, that invisible abode of the Olympian gods!

During his running, the swiftness of Nelson's feet and the velocity of the movements of all his companions (momentarily accelerated to what was perceived as super speed), gave the spectators a glance at what they already suspected to be part of his "alien" powers. They saw what no one else had ever seen before; their curiosity was stirred to an inconceivable degree of frenzy.

At the same time that the flag of the "Universe Outside of Earth" floated in the air depicting blue skies that formed the background for billions of shiny stars, the anthems of many participating nations were enthusiastically heard in the stadium. Then, the Master of Ceremonies officially announced that the International Olympic Committee had voted to name Nelson St★ **"THE DECAMPION!"** This honor was accorded Nelson under a very special flag adorned with a magnificent solar system recreating the radiant light from a sun of first magnitude—a light falling obliquely upon Earth, translucent as golden rays, as an emanation from the skies opening the way for a heavenly apparition. This flag exhibited, as well, the thirteen planets of the solar system still embedded in Nelson's memory which he identified as **PHYLOK**. The thirteen planets beautifully pictured in many different brilliant colors to indicate populated areas. The stunning flag of the "Universe Outside of Earth, . . ." brought to life from the recondite labyrinths of his subconscious mind, had been specifically created by Nelson St★ for this extraordinary occasion. It floated under the blue heavens, bringing together our Earth's globe, in this our Solar System, in this section of the Milky Way, with every globe representing worlds from every other Solar System in the confines of the unknown cosmos!

In addition, under that same flag, it was proclaimed that the nations of this Earth had decided to bestow upon Nelson St★ the titles of "Athlete of the Century" and "Citizen of the Universe" and to confer upon him, also, a special Honorary Doctorate Degree in human relations! A moment proudly shared with Nelson by the President of the Host

Nation representing the heads of all the nations embodying the Olympic world. Global unification had been achieved.

Having completed his last turn around the tracks, and while still listening to the fervent ovation from the frantic crowd, Nelson went onto the special platform that had been set up in the center of the green zone. There, the United Nations' Secretary pinned various medals on Nelson's chest. And while this ceremony was taking place, the Prætorian Guard Commander whispered into Nelson's ears (in a language never heard before on this Earth . . .), the equivalent of the classic Latin phrase: *"Memento homo quia pulvis es et in pulvere reverteris . . ."* ("all glory is transitory!" . . .) Seconds later, Nelson was alone on the special platform, as if on a throne erected for a monarch!

Bowing first in all directions, and with profound concentration of mind that transported his thoughts deep high into space, Nelson St★ closed his eyes. Then, with fervent spiritual reverence that elevated his soul beyond human understanding, he raised his arms toward heaven in a gesture that seemed to indicate either the telepathic unification with other extraterrestrials, or a prayer of thanks. Observing this unusual action, the multitude fell once again totally silent!

Unexpectedly then, lightning and thunder lashed the entire region under a perfectly dry, blue, radiantly sunny sky, as if a menacing storm was approaching. The heavens above and beyond the limits of the oval opening that formed the interior edge of the ring around the roof of the stadium opened, as the iris of a gigantic camera's lens. Nature, then, after moments of agonizing suspense, became very quiet. Peoples' eyes looked up, and around, pivoting on their heads, in an indagatory three-hundred-and-sixty-degree turn watch, searching for an answer, their open mouths describing the parable of the open space. The atmosphere was still dry, and the early afternoon sun was still giving light to

... and warming up ... not only the hearts and souls of every person in that stadium, but scorching the site of the Closing Ceremonies itself. Seconds later however, a sudden, brief, torrential rain, preceded the darkening of the skies. And when the rain had subsided, a diaphanous beam of fulgent colors, containing the complete gamma of the rainbow, but shaped like the shade of a gargantuan electric lamp, streaked out from a newly formed pure white cloud. Then, it stretched its way from high in space, slowly falling down toward the stadium's perimeter where the spectators were simply mesmerized. Here, it illuminated with flashes of powerful light not just the platform on which Nelson still stood, but the whole interior of the stadium. That beam also demarcated the stadium's boundaries with successively fast bursts of splendid white light plasma jets, sealing the oval roof opening with rays of light that simulated a fence's posts. Then, spreading in the form of an ever-enlarging beam, it totally encircled the entire stadium in an inside/out movement, as if the whole structure was a monumental ciborium lit by a gigantic flashlight held from above by the hand of the Almighty! At this point, every spectator, shading widely opened eyes either with bare hands or with any other available object, was able to pierce into the heavens above, getting a unique glimpse at the fascinating brilliant luminosity.

Concentrating on the platform in the center of the green zone, these brilliant rays, moving in a semi-circle (at one time right to left, and at another left to right), as if forming the aperture passage to a vortex spiraling up in the direction of the source of the light, totally engulfed the "hero of the century." Yes; Nelson was engulfed by a translucent curtain that every fan in the stadium, and every television viewer from across the land, was able to glance through. Everyone was able to watch Nelson **transmogrify** himself almost instantaneously into ethereal form first, and then back into corporeal again; and to admire one more moment of the revered "Decampion."

Looking around once again, at this time seeing every person in the bleachers; every seat in the house; every sector of the stadium; every angle, every corner, every alley, at the same time that he turned around . . . and around in a circular motion, along with the platform he was standing on, Nelson thanked the crowd and the authorities; using hand gestures evocative of the ones commonly ascribed to mystics, or to spiritual hermits. With the arms extended half way toward the crowd, he moved both hands in a circular way, from himself toward the multitude, with the thumb and the main fingers of the right hand, and the thumb and the middle finger of the left hand, clasped together. Then, while holding his left hand open over his heart, he extended his right arm in the direction of Cynthia, who sat among the VIPs. Opening his hand as if requesting hers, he invited her with that gesture. Finally, he also made sure everyone heard her name being mentioned over the loud speakers, transmitted telepathically, at the moment he spotted her in the audience.

Smiling with gratitude, but at the same time somewhat embarrassed by the sudden attention given to her in front of millions of people across the communication waves, Cynthia hesitated for a moment. As if reassured by the crowd's applause, she attempted to run toward the middle of the field, but had not fully realized that she would have to go through a veritable maze of athletes impeding her way. About a dozen Olympians, male and female of different nationalities, ran toward her, to offer their help. Showing the courtesy innate to persons with the integrity of character commonly possessed by individuals of their profession, they gently placed Cynthia on their shoulders and carried her onto Nelson's platform in the middle of the most sonorous and pleasing applause by the crowd. There, warmly and tightly embracing the instant they met, they kissed each other—long, tenderly, passionately—a beautiful demonstration showing the Earth, *that there is no need for anything else but love, to bring together not only these two people on this land, but the different peoples of the land, and this Earth's peoples to be, one in essence, with the rest of the universe.* Another, stronger ovation intermittently accompanied by the chanting of both names as a sign of approval by the ecstatic crowd, sealed in that way this unique moment of romance. And at that precise instant the presence of the Teacher at the young age of thirty-seven (not a day older), and dressed exactly the same way she had been so many years back, at the scene of the fire, was spotted among the fans waving good-bye to Nelson. She was seen instants later in successive dissolves, as in scenes from a film, *taking possession of some other females' personalities.* First, the ghost face that appeared to Nelson over the picture frame of his family, in his apartment. Then the face of the woman Nelson had seen when he was in agony during his climbing of what became known as Nelson's mountain. Plus the kind, efficient female nurse, who took care of Nelson at the scene of the accident during the bicycle race. Also, the ghost face of the woman driver whose car had struck Nelson's wife's car, causing the fatal accident that decimated Nelson's family. And looking back, was it really an accident, or simply a pretext for Nelson to be severed from his only Earthly links, with the purpose of affording him the freedom needed for him to live a second life and to achieve success as the Decampion? "Does the end justify the means?" And—is the moral behind applied in the same way outside the limits of our own universe? Not to be forgotten, the one person known to the reporters-cum-sleuths as the "census taker," before showing herself finally as Cynthia at the time when she first appeared to Nelson in the middle of the road where he was on his daily bicycle training routine. Flashed at the proper speed in order to allow the minds of these intrigued spectators to be able to discern just the desired facts, all these women appeared, in retrospect, as the young persons they had resembled at the very first time they were seen, and at the different stages of their lives when they actually were Nelson's subconscious companions, throughout his entire life on Earth. But—as in the apparition, all these women also morphed immediately, one by one, into each other, in a successive dissolve. They disappeared like some of the ghosts seen by Nelson at earlier moments of his life, finally fading into the persona of the beautiful lady, now standing on the platform, indicating that she had been not just Cynthia, not just *Cynthia!*, but all the other women in Nelson's later life as well. (Cynthia was looking today, again, as sensuous and desirable as she had looked at the moment when she had kissed Nelson for the very first time, just before departing from the French chalet style restaurant . . .).

Moments later, and with the majesty and splendor of an angelic vision emanating from the heavens, the intrepid decathlon champion and his companion (whose human identities and origins had never yet been fully established), dissolved slowly into a single, scintillating, magnificent blue St★, the size of a human heart. This unique, extraordinary star was held suspended for some time over the platform while its energy radiated in every direction; spreading it out in flashes illuminating every angle of the stadium; depositing it as "tongues of fire" over every spectator's head; and infusing with that special energy in every heart and mind, a feeling of friendship, of love, and understanding.

After a while both Cynthia and Nelson finally left each other's arms, and each one, individually, still resembled a tiny, brilliant, blue star, and formed, along with all the members of the elite squad of Prætorian Guards, a large cluster of energy manifested as plasma jets of blue tinted light. Then, all faded away . . . by disappearing into the mysterious veil created by the brilliant rainbow from above. Heaven seemed to have opened its gates to allow these "beings" to return to their personal abode. At least that was what the crowd thought they had seen, when they looked up to observe the radiant light from the sky. They saw the athlete of the century, their idol, leaving this Earth in a manner only extraterrestrials are able to perform. The "trainers" and "helpers" who had served Nelson so well, were no longer visible; one by one also, they had dissolved into bundles of bluish light and energy. After having joined Nelson and Cynthia in the rainbow that was still linking the skies above the stadium with the section of Earth within its boundaries, they had also instantaneously vanished from existence. . . . It was as if the Imperial Edict by Constantine The First (the Roman Emperor who dissolved the Prætorian Guard), had been re-enacted at this time . . . in a manner evocative of the present extraordinary circumstances.

The darkness that had fallen upon the stadium had emphasized the beauty of the spectacle. The crepuscular kind of atmospheric conditions brought by the sudden change in weather had served to help reveal not only the magnificence of the view above, but to give a sense of spirituality to the disappearance of Nelson and of Cynthia, both of whom, up until now, had been considered to be as human as everyone else on Earth! A short instant afterward, however, the skies became sunny and bright once again.

Ecstatic, mesmerized by the astonishing beauty of the events at the end of the Closing Ceremonies, yet unable to contain the emotion produced by such a spectacle, the crowd abruptly exploded with a happy expression of its joy, humming along with the Olympian guest singer as he performed Nelson St★'s "The Galactic Hymn."

The shadow of what everyone present in the stadium thought to have been the aliens' space vessel going up, up, and away, is considered, nevertheless, to have been the last vestige of the presence of Nelson St★ in this world. That shadow, receding deeply into space; moving ever so far, far, far away from the Olympic Village; away from the hearts of the spectators in that stadium; now an ever-increasing communicating distance from the millions of viewers on TV (though still connected by the power of the mind, but totally disconnected from the lives of all the inhabitants of Planet Earth), that shadow is what is conceived as the only remaining link between Nelson's Olympus on this Earth, and his spatial abode. That shadow, which after having been discredited by government officials bent on denying the truth, had come to form the idea that everything humans had seen that day had been but a simple mirage created by the impressionable mentality of the fans, is what remains of him, and it is . . . undeniably, in what the soul of humanity believes! Although Nelson did not know it at the beginning when he had said: "There must be some inexplicable reason why my life has been spared so many times before, and . . . more importantly now—because of that I have always believed that I was destined to do something great," the reason for Nelson's second chance in life was indeed his participation in the Olympic Games, culminating with the triumphal ending to his incredible victory, as we humans have already seen. And his "purpose," the unification of all nations on the globe, and of our globe in particular with all the worlds in the cosmos, with the sharing of love, and the rejection of hate, as the only link with other civilizations.

Having achieved both, Nelson had departed the Earth, leaving behind a humanity composed of individuals who now understood and had accepted his mission in this world. Embracing one another, every human being from every ethnic background and every language on Earth proved it so; as Nelson had intended!

With the installation of Nelson St★ as "**The Decampion,**" all nations had come together to recognize the existence of Alien Civilizations . . . and to finally accept their presence on the globe.

In honor of "the First Citizen of the Universe," the triumphant sounds of the "Galactic Hymn . . ." resounded, then, throughout the confines of Mother Earth!. . .

"Sic Transit Gloria mundi!"

Post Script

Who was York Aurel? Why did the government keep in such secrecy his trek to space? Decipher the formula "M.13.En = PHYLOK" (a book by York Aurel whose publication was forbidden earlier by the Government . . .) and you will have the answer to the most extraordinary human adventure in space during the twenty-first century!